The Boys' Life Book of
Football Stories

For several generations, millions of boys all over America have been reading *BOYS' LIFE* magazine, the official publication of the Boy Scouts of America. Now *BOYS' LIFE LIBRARY* presents, in permanent form for all boys to enjoy, this anthology of ten exceptional stories from the pages of the magazine. Readers will find that each story is crammed full of all the drama, humor and excitement of the football season.

The
Boys' Life
Book
of
Football
Stories

Selected by the Editors of *Boys' Life*

Illustrations by Tracy Sugarman

Random House  *New York*

This title was originally catalogued by the Library of Congress as follows:

Boys' life.
   The Boys' life book of football stories, selected by the editors of Boys' life. Illus. by Tracy Sugarman. New York, Random House [1963]
   186 p.   illus.   22 cm.   (Boys' life library, 3)

1. Football stories.   2. Children's stories.   I. Title.

PZ5.B714Bq   63–7834

Library of Congress

Trade Ed.: ISBN: 0-394-80964-5   Lib. Ed.: ISBN: 0- 394-90964-X

Acknowledgments

The publishers wish to thank the following for permission to use these stories, all of which have appeared in *Boys' Life* magazine, copyright 1948, 1950, 1952, 1953, 1954, 1955, 1956, 1957, 1960, 1961, by Boy Scouts of America: B. J. Chute for MASTER MIND, Blanche Gregory for TALKING TURKEY, by Andrew Hall, Wade H. Mosby for DARK, DANK, AND DISMAL, Howard M. Brier for TOUCHDOWN TROUBLE, Caary Paul Jackson for SCARED SCATBACK, by Colin Lochlons, William Heuman for BENCH CAPTAIN, William F. Hallstead for THE BOY WHO THREW THE GAME AWAY, Jay Worthington for ONE-MAN TEAM, Jackson V. Scholz for PIGSKIN PRODIGY, Jay Worthington for HARD-LUCK HAGGERTY.

Contents

The Boys' Life Book of Football Stories

B. J. Chute

Master Mind

If it had happened to any-
one but Irish Mehaffey, maybe it wouldn't have
been so crazy.

Irish is the fullback of the Kent High School
football team, and he is a nice guy and a great
back but very, very dumb. He weighs close to two
hundred pounds, and has bright yellow hair that
stands up like a starched cornfield. We like him
fine, but, as I say, he is not the intellectual type.

Now, I don't consider a knowledge of Greek or
calculus essential to a fullback, but there is one
thing that is essential and, as captain and quarterback of the team, I got pretty worried about it.

Irish couldn't learn signals. You could work out
a foolproof system, and then along would come

Irish and the backfield would knit itself up like an antimacassar, the ball would travel west and Irish would set off east into the rising sun. It wasn't good.

Finally, one afternoon in practice, he really distinguished himself and crashed into his own center. A second-string player picked up the resulting fumble and ran for a touchdown. In a regular game, it would have been simple murder.

That was when I called Chippy Martin into consultation. Chippy is editor of the Kent Weekly and he is fascinated by psychology. He looked at Irish thoughtfully and then said, "The trouble with you, Irish, is you don't concentrate."

"I don't?" said Irish.

"He doesn't even think," I said gloomily.

"Quiet, please—Now, Irish, listen. The human mind is capable of practically anything. All of us vastly underestimate our capacities. The subconscious, for instance, is a controlling force which we seldom use. Do you ever use your subconscious, Irish?"

Irish said cautiously that he wasn't sure he had one. Chippy laid his face in his hands for a moment, but came up swinging. "Exactly. You *don't* use it, and it is a great imponderable force." He stopped off to translate "imponderable," and then went on, reeling off a lot of lovely textbook words. I left them alone, certain it would do no good but willing to try anything once. In fact, I would have been willing to try to put a big pot into a little pot if it would have helped the Mehaffey subconscious.

The next day, in practice, a miracle happened. Irish ran through signal drills like a veteran. I was stunned but as happy as a bookworm in a one-volume encyclopedia, and I patted Irish on the back exuberantly. He looked at me rather oddly. "It seems to work, doesn't it?" he said.

I said that, whatever it was, it worked fine and to keep it up.

"I don't understand it, Jerry," Irish said, "but Chippy says it's a matter of concentration. It's kind of peculiar."

"You just go on being peculiar that way."

He shook his head and said he hoped it was all right. All right? It was wonderful.

Then came Peabody High. I knew in the first ten minutes that Peabody was going to give us a fight. A pint-sized halfback named Jimmy Alfeo ran forty yards, winding up nice and cozy in our end zone. They converted, and it was seven points for Peabody. We settled down to respecting Alfeo and put a cork in that gentleman's activities, so they started smacking us from end to end.

This fine offensive frenzy was rough on their center who was blocking his ears off, and when we got the ball I threw Irish right at him. It was payday for Mehaffey, and he picked up enough yardage to squat us in enemy territory. A pass did the rest, and we scored, tying the game up, 7-7, when the ball sailed over the crossbar. This irked Peabody, and they started tossing the book at us, but we got cagey and play bogged down.

Then, with six minutes to go in the game, Peabody's full bucked almost to midfield again. Two long passes got their ears pinned back, and on fourth down they were on their own forty-six with no future. We spread to receive the inevitable kick.

I went back to safety, and I happened to glance at Irish. He had a most peculiar expression, sort of faraway and baffled as if he was listening to voices, but there wasn't anything to hear. I shrugged and waited for the kick.

All of a sudden, Irish started waving his arms around and yelling for time out. I said to myself, "He's sat on a bee," which was silly because he wasn't sitting and autumn isn't bee-time. But I figured, insects or no insects, desperation had set in, so I signaled the referee.

Irish came racing over like a trumpeting elephant and grabbed me with both hands. "Jerry!" he yelped. "They're going to try a pass!"

I said, "Are you crazy?" Risking a pass, with

the score tied and Peabody in its own home state, would be just the kind of thing that sets the squirrels looking for nuts. I said again, good and exasperated, "Irish, are you crazy?"

He shook his head. He looked kind of solemn. "No. They're planning a Statue of Liberty."

For a moment, I thought he'd played too much ball in too much sun. Then he suddenly shook his head as if he was getting gnats out of his ears. "Gee, I'm sorry, Jerry," he said. "I just had a sort of—hunch, or something. I guess I'm screwy."

I guessed so too, but I whacked him on the shoulder and told him everything was all right and he went back into position. The whistle shrilled. I got all set to catch the punt and figured that with good blocking I might be able to put us in shooting distance for a field goal. I waited.

It was a pass.

It was the Statue of Liberty, that gray-bearded, second-cousin-to-Methuselah, old Liberty play. Alfeo sparked it. We were caught as flat as a pancake under a steamroller.

The scoreboard said Peabody 13, Kent 7. And we never got it back.

I walked home very slowly. If I had played Irish's crazy hunch, we'd have ended with at least a tie. But what quarterback in his senses was going to look for a pass out of a set-up like that? I took a deep breath but it didn't do any good, and then I heard footsteps behind me. It was Irish and Chippy.

Chippy said, "Irish told me, Jerry. About the pass."

I said, "Oh."

Chippy poked Irish. "Tell him what happened, Irish."

"I don't know what happened." Irish looked bewildered. "I was just standing there, Jerry, waiting for the kick, and I didn't have to concentrate on you because there weren't going to be any signals, and so I just happened to concentrate on the Peabody quarterback, and—"

"And?" Chippy prompted.

"And all of a sudden," Irish said unhappily, "it was just like being tuned in on a radio set and I knew he was going to call the pass."

I gulped. Chippy looked at me and nodded very slowly. "That's it, Jerry," he said in an awed voice. "Irish is telepathic."

I said, "That's nonsense!" I think I shouted it.

Chippy reached out a hand and made me stop walking. "Irish," he said, "what's Jerry thinking about now?"

Irish looked at me, and you could see wheels going around in his head. "He's thinking that maybe he's got sunstroke and he'd better go somewhere and have a Coke."

I leapt like a porcupine that's sat on one of its own quills. It was perfectly true. I stared at Irish, and I think my teeth were chattering.

Chippy stared at me. "See what I mean?"

I saw. There was no question about it. Kent High School had a telepathic fullback.

Well, of course, in a way it was wonderful. After all, we knew every play before it came, and the sportswriters called us "the team with the sixth sense." But there was one thing that wasn't wonderful, and that was the way it affected Irish. Every day he got sadder and sadder and his pile-driver line plunges lost a lot of their power. But it didn't matter. We won anyway. The miracle team. The year's sensation. The big Green wave. We couldn't go wrong.

Then, the day before the big game of the season against Pike High, the bottom fell out.

Pike is tradition. If we beat Pike, it doesn't matter what happens the rest of the year, and the corridors at Kent were plastered with signs reading, "Take a poke at Pike," "Make Pikers out of Pike," and "Pike's Peak or Bust."

I was not prepared for what happened.

It was ten o'clock at night and I had just crawled into bed when the doorbell rang. Pop yelled upstairs at me. "Hey, Jerry! Irish wants to see you," and I battled my way into my bathrobe and went down. Irish was sitting on the living room couch.

"What are you doing here?" I asked. "You're supposed to be in bed."

He put his head in his hands. "I know— Jerry, I'm resigning from the team."

I felt as if someone had pulled the room out from under me. "You're *what?*"

"Resigning from the team." He looked like one of those hound dogs that practically burst into tears if you speak to them. "I can't possibly go on playing for Kent with things like this. It isn't— it isn't—What's the word for it?"

All of a sudden, I knew what the word was that he wanted. Maybe it had been kicking around at the back of my mind too. It wasn't ethical to use a telepathic fullback.

"That's the word," said Irish. "Ethical."

I hadn't said it. He'd heard it crashing around in my head. It was unsettling. It was more than unsettling, because, now that I honestly thought of it, it certainly wasn't ethical, and, in that case, what were we going to do? Play Pike without a fullback?

I needed reinforcements, and I walked over to the phone and called Chippy Martin. When I finally got him awake enough to tell him what had happened, there was a short stunned silence. Then he said, "I'll come right over. Just be calm, Jerry. Be perfectly calm."

He was a fine one to go around telling people to be calm. When he came in, he was wearing two unmatched shoes, his kid brother's raincoat and his father's hat. The raincoat sleeves came to his elbows, and the hat came to his chin.

"Irish," said Chippy, even before he got through the door, "you can't *do* this to us. It isn't ethical."

It wasn't a very good choice of words, and, after a minute, Chippy could see it for himself. Irish was perfectly right. We couldn't argue with him. I went out into the kitchen and got some bananas and cookies and we just sat, moody as three black crows, and chewed.

After a while, Chippy said, "There's some way out of this. We can't possibly replace you, Irish. —Look, can you play without being telepathic?"

"Huh?" said Irish, rather quickly. He had just peeled his third banana.

Chippy elaborated. "I mean, you only get the other team's plays when you concentrate on the quarterback, don't you? Suppose you concentrated on someone else, like me on the sidelines. Then what do you think would happen?"

"I'd know what you were thinking. Like now.

You're thinking I'm eating too many bananas and that I'm an awful nuisance and you wish you were home in bed."   .

Chippy winced. "I don't think you're a nuisance, Irish," he said hastily, "and you can have all the bananas you want. They can pop out at your ears, for all I care. PLEASE STOP CONCENTRATING ON ME." After this outburst, he sat still for a moment. "Well, if you thought about me during the game, you'd be all right, wouldn't you?"

Irish said cautiously, "I don't know. I might just accidentally start thinking about the quarterback, and then—"

"Then you'd know the play," I said.

Irish nodded miserably and reached for another banana. I put a cookie in his hand instead, before he started climbing trees and asking for coconuts.

"Well, in that case," said Chippy, "keep it to yourself."

Irish looked at him. "You mean, even if I know what's going to happen, I just stand there and don't tell Jerry?"

"Exactly. When our team's got the ball, you concentrate on Jerry. And, when Pike's got the ball, concentrate on me."

Irish gulped. I gulped. After a moment, Chippy gulped but that was his banana. He wasn't a football player and he didn't see all the difficulties ahead. Still, it was worth trying. I stood up. "You go home to bed, Irish, and forget about this. All you have to do tomorrow is lug that ball. See?"

"I see," said Irish. He sounded as happy and buoyant as a sick clam.

Chippy got up and put on his father's hat. His ears disappeared. "Look," said Chippy, his worst suspicions confirmed, "I've lost weight."

I pushed them both out the door, and then I staggered back to bed.

It didn't rain for the Pike game. The sun came out and the sky was blue and life was one grand sweet song. Or ought to have been. The way I felt, it could just as well have been raining Maltese kittens and St. Bernards.

We had scouted Pike pretty thoroughly. They had a fine team, powerful and fast. Their quarterback, Joe Nesbitt, had quite a reputation, and their ends were flypaper on passes. I knew we'd need Irish to tighten the line and pull them in. I wanted to be able to mix the plays and use everything we had. This was *the* game. I looked at Irish. He was buckling his helmet and talking to himself. I had never seen Irish talking to himself before, and it made me nervous. I went over and touched his arm, and he jumped like I'd hit him with a cactus.

"Oh, hello, Jerry," he said wanly.

"What were you talking about, Irish?"

"Me?" said Irish. "Peter Piper picked a peck of pickled peppers, a peck of pickled peppers—"

I clutched him. "Irish!"

"Huh?"

"Don't *do* that!"

He looked at me reproachfully. "But I have to concentrate on something, Jerry, and Peter Piper helps me keep my mind off Joe Nesbitt and what he's thinking."

"I thought you were concentrating on Chippy."

He shook his head. "I tried that. He thinks too fast. First it's the weather, and then it's the game, and then he starts writing an article in his head, and I get all confused. I thought Peter Piper would clear things up."

I shook my head—it was a fine day for head-shaking and went back into position with my knees playing reveille. We won the toss and elected to receive. It was a beautiful boot, end-over-end, and I pulled it in on the fifteen and started uptown behind good crisp blocking. Irish took his man out cleanly—him and Peter Piper. I began to feel better, and I hit the thirty-eight before I was stopped.

An end run picked up eight yards, and we were knocking at the midfield door. I called Irish on an off-tackle play and he made the down. I gave him the nod again, and he blasted the Pike line for another first. The Kent stands began to shriek. We pulled a reverse and it was like taking candy from a baby. First again, on the Pike thirteen.

"We want a touchdown," yelled the stands. We couldn't miss.

We didn't. In three plays, Irish whammed the ball straight through and, on the last one, he went over the line. Six points for Kent, and the game barely started. I felt colossal. We converted, and Pike was seven in the hole. It was Christmas, and Santa was stuffing our stocking.

Joe Nesbitt returned our kick to the thirty-eight. Two line plunges netted about seven yards. I took another look at Irish, and suddenly I saw him straighten up and look wildly around him. He knows the play, I thought.

Well, so did I. We covered for a pass.

We covered, but the pass was good anyhow. Pike had a first down on our forty-seven, and I could see Irish's lips moving. Pike's next pass was incomplete and nearly intercepted; they tried once more and kicked into the end zone.

That threat had failed. We took the ball on our twenty, and got ready to roll. But Pike was steadying, and what was more they had an eye on Irish. He made about two inches, and then we were set back five yards for an offside. I kicked, and it was first and ten for Pike on their forty-four. They came up over the ball very fast and hit a stone wall. Then the left half found a hole and scuttled through for twelve. A pass was complete on our thirty, and the receiver added seven yards before he was stopped.

Irish's face was all screwed up. He'd known it was coming. I winced all the way through, from helmet to cleats. Joe Nesbitt passed laterally. The half fumbled, and Irish pounced, recovering.

Happy days! I thought. Irish couldn't have known the guy would fumble, so it was heads-up playing that did that one for us, not telepathy. I saw Irish beaming, for a change.

But they slapped our wrists again and we made five yards in three tries, and kicked out of trouble. At least, we thought we were out of trouble. Joe Nesbitt had his own notions and hiked to the forty-seven. First and ten. They pulled a cute play, a fake pass and a run to our weak side. Irish did a funny thing on that one. He started to drive in, suddenly stopped and just stood, looking helpless, with his hands spread wide.

It was almost a twenty-five yard run. I called for time out and went over to Irish. It was like I thought: he'd known the play, blew in to break it up, realized suddenly he wasn't supposed to know it, and stopped practically in mid-air.

This was going to be lovely. I told him to pick

out a clover or something on the field and concentrate on that. He said, "Yes, Jerry" very
meekly, and then added, "Which clover?" I hit
my forehead with my hand and told him to go
back to concentrating on Chippy. However confused Chippy's thoughts were, they couldn't be
any worse than what was happening.

Pike was rolling. It took them two shots to
reach our ten. We stiffened and threw them for a
two-yard loss, and then their right half wrecked
everything with an end run. He downed the ball
back of our goal posts, and it was 7-6.

They tied it up in a bowknot on the kick. The
quarter ended 7-7.

In the second quarter, we played on the see-
saws. Irish was lousy, a word which my English
teacher says he deplores, but if he will find me
another word for what Irish was I'll be happy to
use it. You could see what was happening to the
poor guy. He was always concentrating on the
wrong thing at the wrong time, and it must have
been like chasing ants at a picnic. You scoop
them out of the hot dogs and they turn up in the
thermos bottle. I started longing for the good old
days when nothing had been wrong with Irish
except a genius for mixing signals.

Then, in trouble again on our own twenty-two,
we quick-kicked. Joe Nesbitt fielded and, like a

little gentleman, he fumbled. We recovered by a miracle and were set up in scoring territory once more. I dropped back for a long pass, it settled like a homing pigeon, and the end stepped over the line without a finger laid on him.

The try for goal was short, but the score was 13-7 in our favor.

In the third quarter, Pike took to the air and camped twice in scoring territory but we kicked out of danger. Then an awful thing happened.

With about five seconds to go in the quarter, Nesbitt squirmed and fought his way into the secondary. The play had exploded out of a lateral and caught all of us off balance, including Irish, who had undoubtedly been concentrating perfectly legally on a clover. I saw a startled look spread across Irish's face, and then I saw him spin and start after Nesbitt. Now, Nesbitt is fast, but Irish was coming in on an angle and, by all the laws of mathematics, physics and luck, he had a good chance to cut Nesbitt off his feet.

But Irish slowed down. I actually saw him doing it. His feet stopped hitting the turf and his hands stopped reaching. When he made the tackle, he was wide out, and his shoulder struck air. Joe Nesbitt didn't even have to shrug to clear him; Joe Nesbitt just kept on running.

Kent 13, Pike 13. I called time out, stalked over

to Irish and shook him. "You crazy loon," I sputtered, "what happened to you?"

Irish stared at me. I gave him another shake, like a malted milk. "He's faster than I am," said Irish.

"Who's faster than you?" I yelled.

"Nesbitt."

"Who says he's faster?"

"*He* said so," said Irish, as if that explained everything.

"What do you mean, *he* said so? He didn't say anything—he was running, which was what you should have been doing too."

Irish looked at me forlornly, and then he looked at the ground. "He was thinking it," Irish muttered. "He was running hard and he was thinking he was faster than I was, and I heard him thinking it and I knew he was right, and so I guess I— I just—Jerry, I'm resigning from the team right now!"

All I knew for certain was that there was nobody to replace him. "Look, Irish," I said firmly, "you've got to stay in. There's only one quarter left in the game." I shut my eyes tight and prayed for strength. "Now, listen," I said, "this sounds crazy, but do it anyway. When we've got the ball, concentrate on me. When we haven't got the ball, just don't think at all. See?"

"But—" said Irish.

"Don't think at all," I repeated. "And don't try to do anything. Just get out of the way. Don't try to make a tackle, don't back up the line. *Just get out of the way.*"

He looked at me. I guess he thought I was crazy. I knew I was, but I couldn't see any other answer. He'd be all right on offense if he concentrated on me, because I'd know what he should be doing. But I couldn't nurse him along on defense, never knowing what to expect, and I figured the only safe thing was for him to keep his paws off the whole business. I said, "Don't argue, Irish. Do what I tell you."

He said, "Yes." He didn't have the slightest intention of arguing.

Time out ended, and we lined up for the kick. The stands stopped breathing. Then the whistle shrilled, and Nesbitt booted the pigskin. It lifted in the air, hung for a second over the cross-bar and dropped, safe—14 to 13 for Pike as the quarter ended.

The fourth quarter was most peculiar. Irish did just what I'd told him to; he concentrated on me so hard when we had the ball that his ears must have been stiff, and he never missed a signal. The only trouble was that Pike, with its one-point lead, had no intention of giving ground.

Time ticked its way out. The clock showed two

minutes to go. A sequence of running plays found us near midfield. I thought of a fake center buck and lateral that we had been successful with a few times. It was worth trying. If it flopped, we still had time for a couple of passes that might click.

I called signals. I could almost feel Irish concentrating on me, and I had the consolation of knowing that, anyway, he would get the signals right. The ball was snapped.

And, too late, something clicked in my mind and I saw the play I should have called, the play I would have called if my brain hadn't been all wound up with Irish's. There was a hole big enough to drive a truck through between defensive right tackle and guard. If I had shot a double spinner at that hole, Irish would be on his way.

And then I saw, too late again, what I had done by thinking about the spinner play. Half of me had directed the fake center buck; half of me was mourning over a double spinner that could have been. And, poor Irish, concentrating on both halves, was a split personality.

Completely lost, he tucked the ball under his arm and ran toward me.

I fled. He chased me. The whole Pike team chased him. I raced for the sidelines. I wanted to tunnel my way under the nearest bench and disappear forever, but some reasonable instinct turned me downfield. One lone thought wavered in my shattered brain. I knew I mustn't run toward our own goalposts. "The other goal," I thought. "The other goal!" And then I simply rolled up like an embattled hedgehog and removed myself from the scene.

Irish didn't follow me, because I'd rolled without thinking about it. He was following my mind, not my legs, and my mind was fixed on Pike's goal line.

It wasn't football; that much I'm sure of. It may have been baseball, or water polo. Tiddlywinks, perhaps. It looked like Waterloo. Irish beat a path down the sidelines. Pike pounded after him. I never did know what became of our boys; I guess they just decided to faint in their tracks.

With the Kent stands screaming, Irish stampeded over the Pike forty-yard line, the thirty, the twenty— A Pike runner came up out of nowhere. On the ten, he drew level with Irish. On the three, he hit him. The bleachers rocked with the concussion; I think a couple of clouds fell out of the sky.

Irish fell face down with a mighty thud, stretching for the last precious inch. He wasn't over the goal line.

But the ball was. Kent 19, Pike 14.

He was dazed when he finally sat up, and he was rubbing his head. He said, "What happened?"

I told him. My own head was singing a victory chant and the sun was as bright as firecrackers. I told him what had happened, how first I'd signaled one play and then thought of another and how he'd mixed them together and gone mad. I told him that he'd won the game for Kent.

Irish looked at me crossly and shook his head hard. "What's the trouble with you, Jerry? You're talking through your hat. How could I possibly know what you were thinking?"

I looked at him, and I tried to be calm. It must have been the crack on his head, I thought, and no doubt Chippy would have eighty-two fancy names to explain it. But, whatever it was, Irish Mehaffey, our telepathic fullback, was telepathic no more.

So that's the story. Chippy said that if I wrote it all out on paper it might clear my mind and I'd stop having nightmares.

In the meantime, if anyone can suggest some way to make a fullback learn how to memorize signals, he may write me a letter, outlining his theories. The address is Kent High School.

Andrew Hall

Talking Turkey

The Wednesday afternoon
before Thanksgiving Peeps Elliott right-wheeled
his long, lank form into the locker room of the
Stephens High gym. Spiggot Bates, dear old
George Fawcett Bates, looked up as Peeps plowed
by him shucking his clothes as he went.

"Nice of you to drop in."

"Sorry I'm late." Peeps meant that for the rest
of the squad. He wasn't apologizing to Spiggot
for anything. Peeps and Spiggot were long-time
friendly enemies. The one thing they agreed on
was Drue Matthews, and any wholehearted agree-
ment on the same girl-type person usually leads to
trouble. Their score, however, remained pretty
even. Dish it out and get it back. And this year

they found themselves in the unfamiliar spot of working together as co-captains of the Stephens High football team, and, surprisingly enough, doing pretty well at it, too. Their team was undefeated, with only the championship game to go.

Peeps pulled on his shirt, stuffed it into his pants and started to lace his shoes.

"Listen, guys. Zip says if we don't want Sacksville to think they're playing hop-scotch tomorrow, we gotta smooth out a couple of plays. But remember, it's only dummy scrimmage. We don't dare risk a scratch on anybody. That's important."

He sighed as he said that, knowing how rocked the team would be if they knew what he knew and exactly how important that was. Today it was Top Secret, and he felt it heavy on his shoulders.

"Trying to make like a coach now!" snapped Spiggot. "Just because your old man's a famous coach up at the college doesn't mean our boy Zip needs any help from Ike's little boy in running this team."

"File it, doll," rasped Peeps. He gave a final yank to his shoulder pads and yelled, "Let's go, gang!"

The team jogged out the door and across the lawn of the football field, and Peeps moved over beside Spiggot.

"Look, Spiggot, shape up, will you? We're in trouble."

"Like what?"

"I can only tell you half of it now, but the main point is not to let the team get panicky."

"Why would an undefeated team panic now?"

"I'll level with you right after practice. Will you go along with me?"

Their eyes met and held for a moment. Talk had always been cheap between them, but they really understood each other. Each actually needed the heckling of the other to get the most out of his school life. And Spiggot recognized this as something they had to get together on.

"Okay. Shoot."

"We're using Browsky this afternoon. Corky Davis can't get here."

If Peeps had dropped a hand grenade, he couldn't have startled Spiggot more.

"Corky can't . . . *WHAT?*"

"QUIET! You'll panic the whole works. We use Browsky in dummy scrimmage today. He's not bad. Ike says he's not dumb, he's just slow catching on. Once he gets the strategy, a bulldozer can't stop him."

Spiggot groaned. "We gotta draw pitchas for our center?"

"Maybe not. Come on."

Coach Al Zippe's announcement that Eddie Browsky would work out in the dummy scrimmage with the first string brought a look of horror to every face on the squad . . . including Eddie Browsky's. Eddie was strictly second string, and knew it. He was fair at centering the ball, and his bulk made him a threat as a linebacker. But the guy had a quick, flaring temper, which is not an asset in any sport. He'd go along all right, and then, *whamo!* he'd blow his stack and it was well to keep out of his way until the referee put him out of the game. Eddie was a big boy.

Zippe now tried to pull the team back to its high peak of determination to win this championship. He told them everybody in the high school, in the college and in the town was with them. But when someone asked if Corky would be in the game tomorrow, Zip answered, "You worry about today, son, I'll worry about tomorrow."

The boys turned away heavily to pull off their hooded sweatshirts, and Zippe suddenly snapped, "Hold it! Now get this: Sacksville is rough; they get away with murder. We have a reputation for being good fighters, *clean* fighters, and I'm warning you, if I see any dirty work, even if the refs miss it, *I'll jerk you.* I don't care if we get snowed in the final score, we're going to play decent ball." He looked solemnly around the circle, and added, "That means some of you'll have to slip a snaffle on your tempers. Now get going."

They showed him. Ike Elliott, stopping by as he often did on his way home from Stephens College, murmured to Zip, "They're playing better than they know how. What happened?"

Peeps, on his way to take over the quarterback spot, said sarcastically, "We're the next champs, didn't you know?" and pranced across the field trying to stir up some of the championship steam he was kidding about. As he called the plays and saw the pattern work out, each man where he belonged, blocking, feinting, running the ends, driving through center, his spirits rose and his father's theme song, "You're not licked till the final whistle," started racing through his thoughts. Maybe Ike was right; maybe if they fought right down to the wire, they could wrap this one up, too.

Eddie wasn't doing too badly. Zip had worked patiently with him all year on centering the ball, and he was improving. Peeps and Spiggot explained over and over that once the ball was snapped all he had to do was plow on through and take out the linebacker. Once out of five times the guy accomplished his mission. Good enough for dummy scrimmage, but not for the Thanksgiving game.

Back in the locker room Peeps and Spiggot slammed on their clothes, grabbed their big windbreakers, and hurried out into the crisp November evening. Both of them noted the cloudless sky already bright with stars, and they could imagine the brilliant autumn day that would be part of their last game of the season.

Peeps sighed. "Next time we see those stars we'll either be undefeated or we'll be clobbered."

"That's a tender thought. Is that your FBI report?"

Peeps swung Spiggot around under a street lamp and looked him straight in the eye. "Corky wasn't there today because his arm is bothering him again and he went to have it X-rayed."

Spiggot looked blank. "Is that bad?"

"If they find the elbow is chipped or cracked, it won't be good. Not for tomorrow, anyway."

Spiggot yipped with anguish, and Peeps pulled him along the path. "Easy now. Zip doesn't want anybody to know it—I mean if Corky can't play —until game time. It'll give the guys that much less time to panic."

"So what do *we* do?"

"We got to see Doc Matthews and get the answer. He'll know by now."

Peeps knew how disturbed Spiggot was when his usual ambling gait turned into a jet streak as if trying to show Bannister how it should be done. They rocketed into the Matthews driveway just as Drue Matthews opened the front door and came outside. No need to ask any questions. The bleak look on her usually happy face made them both drop down on the porch with a groan.

"No good, huh?" Spiggot's voice sounded like a cement mixer.

Drue shook her head so solemnly her black curls scarcely moved. "His elbow is chipped and cracked, and Daddy says Corky can't play."

There was an aching silence. Peeps finally dragged his weary body up and started home.

Spiggot asked quietly, "Who do we put in when Browsky blows up and is jerked?"

Peeps stepped back quickly. "Look, I don't have half a plan, but let's keep this top secret until I can talk to Ike. He might . . . Oh, the heck with it." He turned away, then jerked back again. "I don't know why, but let's keep this dark until we've had time to think. Drue, you tell Tod not to tell anybody, and, Spiggot, you call Cork and tell him the same. I'll go talk to Ike and call you."

At home Ike Elliott heard the front door open and came from the kitchen to stand in the dining room archway. His quick black eyes flicked over Peeps, and he automatically straightened his broad lean shoulders. Peeps made no effort to respond to this familiar hint, nor did he sniff hungrily at the rich fragrance of turkey and cranberry that filled the little house.

"Heard the news?" he asked hollowly as he dropped his jacket.

"No, but I don't have to. Corky can't play to-

morrow; you have to use Browsky; when he gets
mad and is jerked you only have Pop Weasel on
the third string, and he can't even hold the ball
yet."

Peeps stared at him. "I thought you hadn't
heard the news."

"I haven't heard anything, but I've got eyes.
I'll tell you what!"

Peeps' head lifted. Maybe this was what he'd
been hoping for. "What?" he asked, and his voice
was two octaves nearer normal.

"*Let's put up a big sign, all over town: OUR
CENTER CAN'T PLAY.* All Sacksville has to do
is SMEAR BROWSKY and they can SMEAR
STEPHENS."

Peeps said, "I thought you were serious."

"I *am* serious." Ike's voice held the familiar
snap to it that yanked Peeps' head erect and
brought Emmy, Peeps' mother, away from her
turkey stuffing. Ike went on. "Of course you don't
need posters. You just walk down the street with
that long face, and word'll get around that
Stephens is licked before they ever kick off. Why
tell 'em? Fool 'em! Worry 'em—at least as long as
you can. And if Browsky can hang on, you might
even . . ."

Emmy, trying to announce dinner, saw a sudden light on her son's face and stopped abruptly
as he went into action.

"Ike! Call Zip and tell him not to leak *anything* about Corky till I see him. Call Spiggot and Scoop Whitelaw and Baby Bunting and Army Armstrong and tell 'em to meet me at Doc Matthews. And do it now!"

Emmy started to squeak something about dinner first, but Peeps was already circling the dining room table on his way to the back door. He grabbed up a pork chop and a roast potato. "Somebody can toss me a salad later," he called, and went on through the kitchen to take a swig from a milk bottle. Emmy yelled a warning not to touch the pumpkin pie set out to cool, and Peeps called back, "Get busy, Ike. That's an order, *Sir*," and was gone.

Ike looked at Emmy blankly. "That crazy mixed-up kid! I hope he knows what he's doing."

Emmy smiled warmly. "He was taught by a great guy. He'll be all right. Start dialing."

Once away from the challenge of Ike's presence, Peeps slowed down and tried on his idea for size. It was pretty feeble, but Ike's "Worry 'em as long as you can" braced him enough to make him enter the Matthews home full of business. The warm tangy odor of mince pies went unnoticed as he brushed by Drue, snapping, "I gotta see your dad, and when Spiggot and Army and Scoop get here tell 'em to wait."

"Well, get you!" gasped Drue. "The boys are

already here, out in the kitchen sampling the Thanksgiving tarts, and if you want to see Daddy, you'll have to hurry before his appointments start, and I'm coming with you."

Peeps laughed at her breathless finish. Things are tough when a guy is so involved he can't stop to admire what the snappy weather does to a girl's cheeks and eyes. "Okay," he said, "I may need you."

After a brief interview with Dr. Matthews, they joined the others. While he put away a short ton of fresh cookies, Peeps outlined what might be their only chance of not being whitewashed.

"Doc says Corky isn't wearing a sling or anything and can get into his uniform. He can do certain calisthenics before the game and he'll even let him be in the kick-off play. Then Zip takes him out, like he's saving him for later, Browsky goes in, and then we start talking turkey to Eddie— *in loud tones.* Tell him he can't play dirty, he can't get mad. Warn him Zip'll jerk him, and he won't win his letter. Tell him if the score gets too heavy against us he'll go out . . . because this is a championship game and we can't fool around. Then we'll say—*loud, remember*—'And if you go out, Eddie, you know who comes in!' You don't ever have to use Corky's name; they'll figure that. And you sure don't have to tell 'em it'll be Pop Weasel. Get the pitch? Maybe, just maybe, they'll

lay off Browsky because they don't want Corky
in there. I said *maybe*." Peeps suddenly slumped.
"I guess it sounds kinda stoopid."

To his surprise the others didn't think it
sounded stupid at all. They quickly organized
themselves and jobs were assigned. Baby Bunting
and Peeps took off to explain the whole deal to
Corky Davis and his family. Scoop lit out to make
certain his father didn't put Corky's injury in the
local paper. Tod went to tell Zip what Corky
could do next day. And Army and Spiggot went
to talk to Eddie Browsky. Drue would get into the
act by leading cheers . . . for Browsky.

Peeps threw a last warning: "Corky'll be on the
bench the whole game, and our job'll be to keep
the Sacks from finding out that he's gotta *stay*
there."

When he got home and began his second dinner, the whole idea did seem pretty stupid. To
Ike's inquiry Peeps said, "Not good, boy, not
good," and would say no more. His spirits were
so low Emmy sent him to bed early, without his
usual help in making a twenty-pound turkey fit
into an eighteen-pound roaster.

At breakfast next morning Ike bowed his head
in real thanksgiving. "Thank you, Lord, for my
good family, my fine community, and my beautiful country. Amen."

And Peeps, loping along to the gym, found

himself thinking of the many families that made up the community, of the many communities that made up the country, and he knew he was proud to be part of it. He somehow pictured families getting together to eat turkey and cranberries and pumpkin pies, but first of all to bow their heads and give thanks for their wonderful country. He guessed that was what Thanksgiving meant.

Coach Zippe came into the locker room just before the boys were ready to start up to the Stephens College Stadium where this holiday game was always played. Tod Matthews helped Corky get into his uniform, following his dad's instructions to prevent further injury to the elbow. Corky's presence seemed to whip the boys into high gear. They were tense and excited but loudly confident in their talk and laughter. And then Zip told them. A funereal silence dropped like a shroud over the entire room. Zip left them with a gravelly, "Do your best, kids. That's all I ask." Peeps and Spiggot exchanged glances and Peeps motioned to Spiggot to take over. Somehow, Spiggot cooked up enthusiasm Peeps knew he didn't feel. Every Stephens man was to act as if Corky Davis was just to go into the game. Nobody, by word or groan or glum face, was to let on that Corky had to stay on the bench. If Browsky could hold his temper and stay in, he'd win his letter. With an apologetic grin at the big center, Spiggot said, "It's the job of all the rest of us to make the guy stay loose so he won't blow his top and get jerked. If our Eddie clobbers somebody, Zip'll pull him out. And then who'll we use?"

"Anybody's mother who'll volunteer to play center will be welcome," bleated Pop Weasel.

The squad laughed and began to talk excitedly about the plan, and Peeps saluted Ike's theory that as long as you're in there trying, the morale is okay.

"Time to shove off, gang."

And forty boys in clean, bright uniforms started the jogging trot up to the college field. Streams of people, moving through the brisk November morning with colors and flowers and megaphones, shouted encouragement to them. Coppy stopped traffic in all directions at the big intersection, waved the squad along, and yelled, "Get 'em, you lugs, or I'll lock every one of you up!"

Peeps stayed close to Browsky and shot out words of caution and advice. He must not get mad . . . he had to hang on to his hot head . . . this was his chance.

Eddie's bass voice boomed, "Me a hero? A likely story!" But he looked pleased, and the others grabbed at that angle and pushed it hard. Corky had more cups and letters than he knew what to do with; this was Eddie's big chance. The hopeful look on Eddie's face gave Peeps a pang of guilt. They'd be lucky if Browsky just centered the ball. Certainly there wasn't any hero stuff in the slow, lumbering guy.

The cheer that greeted the squad as it ran on the field was a frenzied explosion of pride in their past performance and faith in their immediate future. Peeps threw one quick glance at the row of gay uniformed cheerleaders, let it dwell briefly on the one with the black hair, and reflected with pleasure on the big yellow chrysanthemum he had for her to wear to the college game.

"Get with us, Junior," barked Spiggot, and Peeps jumped. That guy never missed a thing.

Play began, and the crowd's din was so deafening both teams often had to indicate they couldn't hear in the huddle. Zip took Corky out right after the kick-off, Browsky went in, and Drue led a terrific cheer for him. Again Peeps felt guilty. Eddie's face was a sunburst of delighted surprise. Hearing his name roared out didn't help him center the ball, however, and Stephens was off to a shaky start. Army and Tod talked to him constantly, and Peeps, not yet in the game, could see the big fellow actually settle down. He also saw that Sacksville, true to form, kneed him, knuckled him, and let him have their cleats any time he was underfoot. Each time Peeps held his breath, and each time he saw Browsky lunge to his feet, thrust out his big lower jaw and, with Tod and Army beside him, miraculously walk away!

That all happened early in the first quarter, and then Sacksville fell into the trap Stephens had set up. Abruptly they changed, and it turned into Be-Kind-to-Browsky Day. Peeps chortled to himself. At least Zip wouldn't have to use anybody's mother.

Stephens played well. They had gone undefeated for good reasons: they were a tight, well-coordinated team, and if Corky Davis had been in there today they could have steamed steadily along to a win—not a pushover, but a win. With a weak center it was tough, but Stephens was holding the score a lot closer than any of those in on the Top Secret had dared hope.

When the score stood at 19-14 the stands began to chant, "We want Corky! We want Corky!"

Peeps, in the quarterback slot now, saw Eddie's face darken, and he urged Tod and Army to keep talking. It did the trick, for on the next play Eddie took out the Sacks' linebacker with an amazingly easy roll. He came up smiling, only to have the smile wiped off by a loud female voice from the stand, bellowing, "It's about time! Now do that again, or I'll come in there and show you how!"

Eddie Browsky's eyes met Peeps', and he said sheepishly, "That's my mom, and don't think she don't mean it, either."

The thought flashed through Peeps' mind that other families besides the Elliotts cared how their kids made out; then his eye caught the clock. Time was short and one, just *one*, measly touchdown would give Stephens High the unbelievable win . . . the championship! But how? Their best play, a reverse around end, had been consistently messed up by a fast Sacksville halfback. Their drive through center usually ran into a stone wall that was the linebacker. Responsibility for both was actually Browsky's, but Peeps knew the guy was doing his best . . . even better.

Unexpectedly Browsky came up to him in the huddle and said, "Look, I been thinking."

Peeps looked and realized that on Eddie it showed.

"I been figuring, and I say call 31 for the next play and for Pete's sake don't lose the ball. Then next, start 31 and end up 48."

Peeps opened his mouth, but Eddie said, "If they don't call for time out after the next play, the 31 I mean, I'll quit thinking. Honest."

Just then the whistle blew, and Stephens was penalized five yards for delaying the game. Peeps groaned. What a dope he was! But . . . he had no better idea, so he called for 31.

As he waited for the ball, Peeps could hear
Browsky's bass voice. He couldn't get what he was
saying but he saw Tod and Army jerk their heads
up in surprise. Old Eddie's voice rumbled on, the
ball was snapped, they went through center, and
Stephens was stopped cold.

Peeps set his teeth in rage when to his utter
surprise Sacksville did call for time out. Eddie
gave him a broad grin, and Peeps reluctantly decided to go along. It was too late to set up anything else. He'd try it, a feint through center and
a handoff for an end run. He called 31-48, they
lined up; and again Peeps could hear Browsky's
voice. The ball was snapped, and after that Peeps
was never quite sure what happened. They made
a feint through center, Scoop Whitelaw took the
handoff, streaked around right end, and went
over for a touchdown, standing up!

All Peeps knew after the play started was that
the stands went wild, Stephens scored, two Sacks
were slow getting up, and Eddie Browsky stayed
flat on the ground. Peeps rushed to him and
found that, aside from cuts and bruises, he'd only
had the wind knocked out of him and soon was
on his feet. He gave Peeps a wobbly grin. "That's
what I get for thinking."

Higby, who hadn't missed kicking the point all
year, booted it wild, but nobody cared. Peeps just

begged the team not to let anybody go anywhere with that ball. Hang on . . . hang on . . . The final whistle blew, and the referee threw the ball into the air!

The place exploded with joy; the whole Stephens stand was a whirling mass of color; the cheers for Scoop were deafening; and a tired, slap-happy team ran for the locker room. But Peeps felt as if he had been reading a mystery, and the last pages were missing. They'd won, sure they'd won, but *how?* What happened? They'd tried that end play a dozen times before. Suddenly it worked. How come?

He got the story, as he dressed, from Tod and Army and battered old Eddie. Right at the end Eddie had suddenly spilled the Top Secret to the enemy. He'd roared right in their faces, "You guys have been real sweet to me all day so they won't put Corky in. Well, I'll clue you. Get this, you lugs: Corky *can't* come in. He's got a busted funny bone, and he can't get off that bench. Not for nothing. Take me out, and they'll have to put my mother in. That's all we got. Now shall we dance?"

Eddie explained. "Maybe I shoulda figured it sooner, with them two guys messing up our plays. I figured if I sucked 'em in, you know, made 'em sore because we'd fooled 'em all morning, they'd

really try to double-team me." He guffawed, then grabbed his swelling jaw. "I figured if I went limp, they'd crash and knock each other out. I ain't so good at brain work—I kinda forgot I'd be in the middle."

Just then the cheering section cut loose outside the locker room windows. "We want Scoop! We want Scoop!"

Suddenly Scoop grabbed someone who had clothes on and shoved him toward the door. "Go tell 'em! Tell 'em all I had to do was walk over the line. Tell 'em about Eddie. Eddie won the game!" The boy took off, the crowd silenced, and then came a cheer for Browsky that rocked the building.

Peeps glanced at Eddie and saw that the big guy's dream of a lifetime had come true. Eddie Browsky was a hero. As the tremendous roar of voices dropped, one, loud and female, was clearly heard. "No turkey for you, Eddie boy! Momma'll give you the biggest steak this side of Texas."

Eddie grinned at Peeps. "That's my mom, and don't think she don't mean *that*, either!"

Wade H. Mosby

Dark, Dank, and Dismal

At the start of the season the sportswriters were having their usual ball about what a terrific team we were going to have at Colton Tech.

From last year, we had halfbacks George Darkner and Vlad Dankowicz. George Abbis was a letterman at quarterback, and I figured to do as well as any at fullback. Maybe you remember me—Kevin O'Brien—from last year's third team?

Anyway, our line wasn't too bad, and against the scrubs it could open holes big enough to stampede elephants through. Sideways. After the first week of practice, the whole campus was buzzing that this was the year we were going to beat State.

Well, we were as surprised as anyone when Melton College and Seminary beat us, 7 to 0.

The next week Crandon College won by a touchdown, and Abbis got a leg fracture that put him out of action for the rest of the season.

After the first game, someone had started calling the backfield "Dark, Dank, and Abbismal," but with Abbis out, they changed it. That's how I got my nickname, "Dismal" O'Brien.

Our big trouble, we had learned, was lack of depth. The reason we ripped through the second team so easily was not our speed, elusiveness, and talent, as the sportswriters had been saying, but the scrubs' ineptness, sincere desire to avoid collision, and complete lack of guile. Which meant that every time we ran in a substitute, it was like putting out a welcome mat with directions to our goal.

Curly Balducci, the coach, got to talking to himself, and what words he had left over for the rest of the world weren't exactly reserved for summit conferences.

On Tuesday night after the Crandon game, we were trying to adapt our defense to some Institute plays our scouts had brought in. We did fairly well, but got caught flat-footed on a quick kick. It was a dandy. Went spiraling right off the field and came down just aft of the slide trombones over where the marching band was practicing. This naturally disrupted marching a bit. Coach ran over to the sidelines.

"All right," he hollered in that sarcastic way of his. "This isn't the Polo Grounds and you don't get to keep fly balls hit into the stands. Now throw it here!"

Some guy in the middle of the band picked up the ball and gave it a flip. I'm still not sure I believe what happened next. That ball didn't get much more than 10 feet of altitude at best, but it didn't seem to need any more than that. It came blistering along as if it had a mind of its own.

Balducci was standing there with his hands on his hips, probably trying to think of something else to holler at the band, when the ball caught him right between the eyes. He sat down. Hard.

A couple of us helped him to his feet. Coach turned to Aqua Watt, the manager. "Aqua," he said in a trembly voice. "I want the guy who threw that ball. Dismal, you be there, too. My office in ten minutes. That's all for the rest of you for tonight."

Well, I could see that he might want to chew out the chucklehead who fired the bean-ball, but I couldn't think of any reason why he should be sore at me. Anyway, I showered and dressed in a hurry and got up to Balducci's office in about eight minutes. Aqua Watt was already there with this guy in the band uniform.

"You can go, Aqua," Coach said. And Aqua did. "Sit down," Coach said to the band guy, and he did. "What's your name?"

"Knocklemeier, sir," said this kid. "Philip A."
He was about 5 foot 9, and probably didn't weigh
160 wearing a French horn.

"What course are you taking?"

"Music, sir. And sociology. Sir, I'm sorry I hit
you. The light was a little bad or I guess you
would have caught the ball."

"Never mind that," Coach said. "What do
you play in the band?"

"The glockenspiel, sir."

"The . . . ah, yes," Coach said. "Well, Glockenmeier, I want you to do something for me."

"Knocklemeier, sir. Philip A."

"Oh, sure. Well, Knockle . . . , ah, Phil. I want
to see you toss a football a few times."

So that's where I came in. Knocklemeier,
Coach and I went down to one end of the field,
and Coach had Knocklemeier toss passes to me.
The guy was uncanny. He seemed to use no more
effort than a guy swatting a fly, but those passes
of his would come steaming to me no matter
where I was. If it was in the flat, I'd run a few
steps, turn, and there it was. Same thing for longs,
shorts, or you name it. You didn't have to split a
spleen reaching, either. All you had to do was defend yourself, because if you didn't catch the ball,
it would hit you on the head nine times out of ten.

"That's enough," Coach said finally. "Knucklespiel, I want you to suit up for practice tomorrow night."

"Knocklemeier, sir," the kid said. "I'd like to, sir, but I'll be busy tomorrow night."

"Busy doing what?"

"It's the last band practice before the Institute game, sir," said Knocklemeier. "Director Billingsley is counting on me. This is the first year he's had a glockenspiel in the marching band, and we have worked out a few numbers for the half time show."

Coach's chin dropped and he stared at Knocklemeier as if he were a subversive that had just popped up with the toadstools. In a minute he got a grip on himself.

"I'll speak to Billingsley about practicing your number early. Report here at 4:30."

"Yes, sir."

The next night we just ran through signals in preparation for the Institute game. Knocklemeier looked sort of clumsy in a suit, but he tossed a few more passes for Coach, and he could kill ducks with that football.

I walked home with him—he lived near the Delta Gam house—and found out that he came from a little town where they played six man football. They played the game for fun, and put a lot of passing and razzle dazzle into it.

Phil was a sophomore. He hadn't gone out for

football at Colton because he wanted to concentrate on his music. He didn't think he'd like the eleven man game, anyway.

"You spend a couple of hours out here every night, and you're too tired to study," he said.

I thought about it that night.

Knocklemeier suited up for the Institute game, but Coach didn't put him in. He let him change into his band uniform in plenty of time to play the glockenspiel at the half, and you'd think that hc had scored four touchdowns, he was that happy. He came back to the locker room with his glockenspiel, which was a sort of one lung xylophone, and knocked off a few numbers for us. We needed cheering up, because Institute had scored and we hadn't.

But Knocklemeier seemed so interested in his music and so unconcerned about the score that the rest of us realized that the world wasn't coming to an end. I'm not saying that this was responsible, but we relaxed in the second half and scored three times. Institute didn't gain more than 20 yards the entire half.

Knocklemeier reported for football practice Monday with a long face. He told Coach that the glockenspiel number had been dropped from the marching band. I saw Balducci look a little guilty, but Knocklemeier didn't suspect anything, and started learning to block, run, and tackle with the same intensity I imagined he had given to his music.

That was the worst week of the fall. Balducci drove us until we could hardly get off the field. I expected the kid to break in half, but he was as wiry as a fraternity sofa. By the time we left for Wilson College Friday night, he knew what was expected of the quarterback. Balducci had poured the pass plays into him, and he was familiar with our basic running game.

Wilson was supposed to be the weak sister of the conference, but with the home fans hollering their heads off that Saturday afternoon, the Wilsons fought like a pack of panzers. They couldn't score on us, but we couldn't get inside their 10 yard line either.

Midway in the last quarter, Balducci put Knocklemeier in. We worked up a first down on Wilson's 30 with a series of running plays. Then Sousa hit our right end, Dick Petersen, right on the Adam's apple with a pass. Petersen, with not a soul near him, dropped it.

The Wilson line guessed right away that Knocklemeier was a passer, and when he faded back on the next play, every Colton receiver was covered. The kid had to eat the ball 20 yards behind scrimmage.

We tried the same play, only this time I nailed the tackle who caught Knocklemeier before.

Again all the receivers were covered. I picked myself up and hollered "Run!" The kid took off after me and while the Wilson backs tried to shift gears, Knocklemeier hot-footed it to their 10. I made eight yards on the next play, and Dank smashed into the end zone. Darkner converted, and the game ended that way, Colton, 7; Wilson, 0.

Balducci was plenty happy. Knocklemeier had looked good carrying the ball, we had won—and the State scouts certainly hadn't found out what a passer the kid was.

The newspapers didn't consider us a wisp of a risk to State's unbeaten team. The only argument was about whether Colton would be able to last through the game.

Each member of the squad felt that the condescension was aimed at him, and each man executed his role as if the Grim Reaper himself were waiting to reward the slackers.

Saturday was made to order for a pass offense, clear and dry with only enough wind to keep the stadium flags from drooping. Balducci started Knocklemeier at quarter. I was to call the plays in the huddle. I figured Coach wanted to run up a score as fast as possible and then protect his lead. There's a psychological advantage in scoring first if you're the underdog. It puts the pressure on the big boys, and when they start trying too hard, they tense up and make mistakes. When we trotted onto the field, I don't think a man in a Colton uniform doubted that we would win.

State won the toss and elected to receive. I chose to defend the south goal, although the choice was meaningless. Darkner's kick was returned to State's 32, and the game was under way. State lost three yards in three running plays, and then punted to Dankowicz on our 25. I saw him tuck the ball under his arm and head north, and I threw a block into a State end bearing down fast. While I was picking myself up, I heard a sudden roar from the crowd. Dank had fumbled. State had recovered.

Here was the break, but it had gone the wrong way. State caught fire. We looked for a running play on their first down, and a pass in the flat caught us looking on vacantly like a delegation of visiting heifers. The State end didn't even get a fingerprint on his trousers as he trotted into the end zone. The conversion was good, and as we moved back to line up for the next kick-off, I saw that Balducci's shoulders seemed to have joined his elbows in his raglan sleeves.

We picked up a few yards on running plays, and Knocklemeier clicked on a couple of passes, but we couldn't keep up a sustained attack. We were the ones who were tense and pressing, and things wouldn't go right for us. Only Darkner's inspired punting kept us out of trouble in the first half—that and savage play by our linemen.

Just before the half ended, the State band lined up behind our goalposts, and as we walked toward the locker room, I saw Knocklemeier watch fascinated as the band marched onto the field. It had a whole squad of glockenspiels. Well, four of 'em, anyway.

Balducci didn't have much to say. He just told us to keep doing our best. We felt pretty bad, and just sat there, too big to cry, too sore to laugh. Coach leaned near the door, his chest caved in, looking glum.

Then the door opened, and in skidded Knocklemeier, whacking away at one of the State glockenspiels.

"Get a load of this instrument, Dismal," he said, trotting over to me without noticing the coach. "State has three others just like it. Their director let me try this one."

"Maybe he'll lend the others to the rest of our backfield," Balducci broke in.

Everybody guffawed, except Knocklemeier, who looked a little embarrassed.

"I'll take this back now," he said.

"The heck you will," Balducci snorted. "Hey, Aqua. Take this xylophone out of here. And you, Knocklemeier, hereafter come straight to the dressing room at the half. They don't need you out there in the grounds crew."

Someone hollered in the door that we were due on the field, and we ran out into the sunlight still chuckling over Knocklemeier and the coach.

Darkner ran the kick-off to State's 40. I got 10 yards off tackle, and Dank got another eight with a delayed buck. The State backs still were trying to figure what had happened to their defense against our ground game when Knocklemeier rifled a pass to Ken Eaton, our left end, that went for a touchdown. Darkner's kick was wide, but we felt that we were on the way.

As it turned out, our touchdown inspired State, and at the end of the third quarter they led us, 14 to 6. Darkner twisted his knee on the first play of the fourth quarter, and had to be helped from the field. Ed Thorson, who replaced Dark, was fair on defense, but he couldn't punt for sour apples. Knocklemeier read my mind. We couldn't kick out of trouble any more.

"Send 'em deep, Dis," he said, and I decided to give it a try.

On the next play Eaton and I went deep. Knocklemeier's pass dropped into my arms, and we made 25 yards. We tried the same play at the other end, and the State safety man was lucky to break it up. I saw that State's backfield had loosened up, and called for a couple of shovel passes over the line. Knocklemeier couldn't miss.

We scored on a pass to Dankowicz. Thorson attempted the conversion, but missed by five yards. We now trailed by just two points.

But that two point margin might as well have been 50 points when we looked at the clock. There were three minutes left, when we finally had our hands on the ball again.

I called for the deep pass on our first play, and it clicked again, with Eaton carrying the ball out of bounds on State's 45. I started to call for the short passes, just over the line, when Knocklemeier interrupted me.

"Dis," he whispered. "I can't pass. That big tackle fell on me and I can barely lift my arm."

If Knocklemeier went out, State wouldn't worry about passes and our ground game would be stopped. If he stayed in, even without passing, we might be able to keep them off balance.

Thorson took the ball on a hand-off from Knocklemeier on the next play, and Knocklemeier faked the State line into chasing him to midfield. Thorson went to State's 20 before their safety man nailed him. On three more running plays, we picked up six yards, and, with the clock running out, I dragged out Old Desperation.

OD was a fake field goal attempt. Knocklemeier was in kicking position and I was the holder.

The gimmick was for me to keep the ball and either pass or run. It was a play you can't pull more than once a season, and you're lucky if it works once in five seasons. This started out to be one of those no-working times.

Garrott, our center, was weary, maybe. Or maybe he forgot the play. Anyway, when the ball was snapped, it whistled right past my outstretched fingers and into Knocklemeier's hands. With the State line charging in, he couldn't get into position to lateral. He couldn't pass, and a run would be suicide.

Without hesitation, Knocklemeier dropped the ball, and as it touched the ground he kicked it soundly. It soared squarely between the goal posts.

The officials had to confer for several minutes before they announced that the dropkick, though a bit moldy these days, still was a legal scoring weapon and worth three points if successful. When the gun sounded a moment later, the scoreboard read: State, 14; Colton, 15.

Balducci was so happy I thought he was going to cry in the locker room.

"Glockenmeier," he bubbled, "why didn't you tell me that you could dropkick like that?"

"Why, Coach," said Knocklemeier, "you never asked me."

"Guess I didn't at that," grinned Balducci.

"Well, we'll certainly show 'em next year, with your arm in shape and that toe of yours."

"I meant to tell you about that, too, Coach," Knocklemeier said. "I won't be out for football next year."

"What do you mean?" asked Balducci, looking stricken.

"I'm going to transfer to State."

"But you'll lose your eligibility for the season!" Balducci trumpeted.

"Not for the marching band," said Knocklemeier. "They've asked me to play first glockenspiel next fall."

He did, too.

Howard M. Brier

Touchdown Trouble

Ravenna called for time out in the closing minutes of the game with Airport High.

Turk Bailey, Ravenna's 190-pound fullback, had his wind knocked out, and he was lying on the 40-yard line with a little huddle of players around him. Coach Murdock was bending over him, loosening his belt.

Peewee Perkins, quarterback, took off his helmet and rubbed the sleeve of his jersey across a grimy, sweat-streaked forehead. He stood alone, hunch-shouldered and disconsolate, studying the scoreboard at the end of the field.

There was the whole sad story in bold letters and numbers. *Airport High 18: Ravenna High 0.*

Fourth Quarter. The clock was stopped with three minutes of playing time left.

It was hopeless. Peewee felt sick, and his face showed it. This was the seventh game of the year, and Ravenna High was getting smeared again. The entire season had been a series of humiliating disasters.

Trouble had started even before the first game. Andy Mullins, first string quarterback, had broken his collar bone in pre-season scrimmage. Ravenna had pinned a lot of hope on Andy's educated arm. Sportswriters had predicted the Ravenna Bulldogs would pass their way to another championship. That sounded silly, now, with six defeats and a seventh on the way.

Peewee Perkins had tried to fill Andy's shoes, but no one in this league could pass a football like Andy. Peewee felt responsible for the miserable showing Ravenna had made.

Sam Chambers looked at Peewee, started to say something, then thought better of it. What could you say to a guy like Peewee, who played his heart out and still couldn't win?

Turk Bailey knew that Peewee was not entirely to blame. Turk was getting uncertainly to his feet. He glanced at the scoreboard, and then at the quarterback. A resigned grin crossed his thick lips.

"Guess we can't win 'em all, Peewee."

"We can't lose 'em all, either," Peewee said, as the men gathered for the huddle.

"I'm not so sure," Turk returned. "Only one game left, an' that's against Forest High. It'll be slaughter."

Peewee bit his underlip. What chance did Ravenna have against the powerful Forest team, when little Airport High was pushing them around like lawn mowers? Airport had won two and lost four. It would soon be three wins for Airport. This was the game Ravenna should have taken.

Peewee called for an off-tackle play, with Chambers packing the ball. Chambers smacked into a swarming mass of Airport players, and he was down at the scrimmage line. It was fourth down, and eight to go. The ball was on Ravenna's 40-yard line.

In the huddle, Peewee looked at the bruised and battered faces that circled him. Rutledge had a black eye that was swollen half shut. Dutch Morgan had a cut lip that was bleeding. Buzz Wilson was limping. Defeat was written on every face. Peewee called a pass play.

"It's fourth down," Chambers said.

"Yeah, I know," Peewee returned. "Number twenty-six. Bayles and Dennison—get down fast. It's our only chance."

They were slow coming out of the huddle, and

the officials penalized Ravenna. Peewee still insisted on the pass.

With the play in motion he had a feeling that this last attempt was also doomed. Two Airport linemen were on him, but he managed to shake loose. Peewee ran toward the sideline, scanning the distant goal for a man in the open. Dennison, right end, was all tied up, but Tod Bayles was clear. Peewee heaved the ball—a long, down-field pass. His aim was good, and the ball reached its mark, but Tod Bayles juggled it for a moment on his finger tips, and the ball slithered away to bounce crazily on the 10-yard line.

The clock stopped with two minutes to go. Ravenna had booted another chance. The touchdown trouble that had dogged this team since early fall was still robbing them of victory.

Airport High took over on the Ravenna 40-yard line, and they carried it to the twenty before the gun sounded ending the game.

The Ravenna team straggled off the field, weary and dejected, broken in spirit. The team that had been lauded as having title possibilities was tasting bitter defeat. Little Airport High had lowered the boom on them, and Ravenna's humiliation was complete.

Tempers were short in the shower room, and there was bickering and loud talk. Players who had started the season with great ambitions were growing surly, and blaming others for shortcomings that should have been shared.

Peewee showered quietly in a corner, and listened to the excuses and accusations being tossed about. It was all wrong. These fellows were good players. They had demonstrated that in previous years. This team could have been a great team, but it had fallen apart. Each week it had played worse than the week before, and the following Saturday Ravenna would meet the strongest team in the league. Forest High was undefeated, and gunning for the title. If this was despair, the Bulldogs would hit bottom when they met Forest. It would be murder—just plain murder.

Peewee was deep in thought while he pulled on his clothes. He walked home with Turk Bailey.

"Have you ever seen such a loused-up season?" Peewee asked.

"Couldn't be worse," Turk replied. "What makes me sore is that everything might have been different. We have practically the same team as last year, and they didn't make apes out of us then."

"I suppose I'm to blame," Peewee said.

"What makes you think so?"

"If Andy Mullins hadn't broken his collar bone he'd be playing quarter. Andy can pass, and he has brains."

"You're smart enough," Turk said. "Of course

Andy would help any team. We've missed his passing arm, but even without him we should have made a better showing. Look at us now— fighting to keep out of the cellar."

"There's too much beefing going on. You heard that talk in the shower room. Something is terribly wrong with this team."

"It's just nerves—tension."

"A team can't play ball when the players are fighting among themselves. What can we do to get this gang together again?"

Turk Bailey shrugged.

"That's not in my department. You're the master mind of this outfit. You figure it out. But if you ask me, it's too late."

Peewee Perkins spent a restless night trying to study, but he found his mind drifting to the gridiron, and the coming game with Forest High School.

He got up from his study desk and paced the floor, stopping now and then to survey himself in the full-length mirror on his closet door.

Peewee was not as small as his nickname might indicate. He was a stocky 160 pounds, and he had always dreamed of being a football player. He had played two years on the Ravenna second team, and no one had paid much attention to him. It was only after the accident to Andy Mullins that he got his chance.

The thrill of that big opportunity had long since worn off. There had been no 70-yard gallops for a touchdown, no brilliant passes in the closing minutes to snatch victory from defeat. Just discouraging, heart-breaking football, that brought plenty of bumps and bruises, but no glory.

Peewee knew that the desire for recognition was the driving force that kept all football players slogging along through rain, and cold, and mud. It was like a flame burning deep within. When success came, the flame burned strong and bright; with failure it flickered dim, but never quite went out. Right now the flame was sputtering feebly in the heart of every Ravenna player.

Peewee stood in front of the mirror, hands on hips, scowling slightly. His imagination turned the glass into a sort of dreamlike television screen, and for a moment he saw himself pounding, slashing, driving, bounding like a startled antelope through a welter of Forest High players. There was a football tucked in the crook of his arm, and with amazing broken-field running he was eluding all tacklers. With a final blast of speed he crossed the last white line and pranced into the end zone. The crowd went wild. He could hear them yelling. "Peewee! Peewee!"

Then the illusion of his dream was shattered.

Someone was calling "Peewee!" but it was only his kid sister downstairs.

Peewee went to the hall and leaned over the bannister.

"What do you want?" he snapped, irritably.

"Telephone. How many times do I have to call you?"

"Okay. Okay. I'll get it up here."

Peewee lifted the receiver on the extension phone. It was Marybeth Townsend, a girl he had taken to a couple of school dances.

"Hello, Peewee?" Marybeth said, a note of excitement in her voice.

"Yeah," Peewee replied.

"I have some terribly important news," Marybeth confided. "My uncle is coming to the Ravenna-Forest game next Saturday."

"Yeah? So what? Who's your uncle?"

"He's assistant football coach at State. He's coming to scout the game, but he doesn't want anybody to know about it."

Peewee was silent for a moment while this confidential bit of information soaked in.

"If it's so secret," he said, finally, "why are you telling me about it?"

"It isn't that secret. It's just Uncle Ralph doesn't want any fuss made about it. He's coming to watch the Forest team. He's heard about two or three Forest players who might be interested in going to State next year."

"More power to him," Peewee said. "Hope he gets 'em."

"Thanks, Peewee. I just thought you might be interested."

"Sure. I'm interested. Thanks."

Marybeth switched the conversation to school and lessons and she rattled on for thirty minutes, but Peewee heard only part of what she was saying. Most of the time his mind was toying with an idea that had come to him since learning of the expected visit from the college coach. Finally the conversation ended.

"Be seein' you."

Peewee returned to his room and stretched out on the bed. This idea had possibilities. He kicked it around from several angles, and it gradually evolved into a clear-cut plan. His mouth spread in a wide grin. Marybeth's information might be helpful.

Football practice on Monday and Tuesday was ragged. Coach Murdock, sensing the depths to which morale had fallen, made a valiant effort to lift the spirits of the team, but it seemed useless. The players went through scrimmage like sheep herded from one spot to another. There was no drive, no fire. Disgust was apparent on Murdock's face—and frustration.

A sportswriter who had come to watch the workouts on the long chance there might be something favorable to report, summed up Ravenna's chances in one word, "Hopeless."

After the Wednesday turnout, Peewee walked home with Turk Bailey again.

"We might as well forfeit the game," Turk said. "We aren't even playing in the same league with Forest High."

"I'm not so sure of that," Peewee replied.

Turk looked at the quarterback, surprised.

"You know we haven't got a chance."

"There's always a chance."

"What's eatin' you? Get hit on the head, or something?"

"Nope. I have a plan."

"A plan for what?"

"A plan to lick Forest High on Saturday."

"Now I'm sure of it. You're off your rocker."

"If you and Sweeney will come to the house tonight, I'll tell you about it."

"Why Sweeney?"

"Because he plays center. Only three of us will know this plan—the fullback, the quarterback, and the center."

Turk scratched his head, and looked at Peewee skeptically, but that evening he and Sweeney reported on time, and the three went into a huddle in Peewee's room. It lasted two hours, and when the meeting broke up Turk Bailey and Sweeney were grinning. Peewee had sold them a bill of goods.

Saturday came with a gray umbrella of high cloud, but there was no rain. The turf was solid under foot, and the air was calm. It was ideal weather for a late fall football game.

The Forest High stands filled early, for this was their final game of the season. Forest led the league with seven wins, and they were a cinch for the championship. The student body had built up enthusiasm that was almost fanatical for their green-shirted warriors. Even before their team was on the field their school song was booming across the gridiron, "Bow Down to Forest High."

The words of the song, muted by distance, drifted through the windows of the dressing room where the Ravenna players were donning their uniforms.

Coach Murdock, moving among his players, seemed to sense in a vague way that something was different about this team. Peewee saw him standing near the shower room door, head cocked on one side, and a quizzical expression on his face.

The Ravenna players were dressing silently. The usual pre-game banter was missing. Hal Adams, who generally sat pounding the palm of his hand with his fist to let off nervous energy, was seated quietly on the bench, staring at the cleats on his football shoes.

Sam Chambers, who often indulged in horse-play before a game, stood by himself soberly lacing his shoulder pads. Tod Bayles and Pete Dennison, ends, were not tossing wisecracks back and forth. Instead they sat tongue-tied waiting for the signal to take the field.

Dutch Morgan and Buzz Wilson, guards, stood near the door. Dutch was adjusting the chin strap on his headguard. Often before a game he talked loud and fast to ease the tension, but today no words crossed his lips. The same quiet determination was exhibited by Rutledge and Crowell, tackles.

Finally, Coach Murdock ran his fingers through his hair.

"What goes on here?" he said. "You fellows act like you're going to a funeral."

"We are," Peewee said, seriously. "Forest High's funeral."

Coach Murdock's mouth dropped open. In twelve years of coaching he had never been confronted by a situation like this. For the first time he was stumped.

"Okay," he said, at last. "I hope it's their funeral, and not yours."

The Ravenna team took the field.

Peewee, Turk Bailey, and Sweeney were the last to leave the dressing rooms.

"Did you get that mail off Thursday?" Turk asked.

"Yeah," Peewee replied.

"Think it'll work?" Sweeney asked.

"It's already working," Peewee said.

A half-hearted yell came from the Ravenna stands as the blue and gold players trotted out on the turf. The Ravenna student body had watched this team muddle through seven games, and there had been little cause for cheering during the season. Now, only the most loyal fans remained, and they had come expecting defeat.

After the warm-up, the referee called the captains to the center of the field. Turk Bailey stepped forward for Ravenna. He won the toss, and elected to receive. Forest chose to defend the west goal.

Up in the radio booth an announcer was preparing his listening audience for some kind of mayhem.

"The teams are moving into position now. The green-suited players from Forest High will kick-off. As you all know, Forest has won every game this season by a comfortable margin, and the Ravenna players have yet to show anything in the way of offensive power. No team has been able to stop Coach Benson's scrapping Tigers, and it is doubtful if the Ravenna Bulldogs can turn the trick. They're set to go now, folks. The referee signals the captains. Both teams are ready. There's the whistle. There's the kick . . . a high end-over-end boot that is coming down on the Ravenna 10-yard line. Sam Chambers is under it. He has the ball. He's swinging to the left. He eludes two tacklers. He cuts back. Now he's in the clear. He crosses the twenty . . . the thirty . . . say, that boy Chambers is turning on the steam . . . the forty. Wade, right tackle for Forest, snagged him on the forty. He's down on the forty-two. It will be Ravenna's ball, first and ten, on their own 42-yard line. That was a nice return Chambers made. Thirty-two yards on the first play of the game. Ravenna is in the huddle now. . . ."

"Nice going, Sam," Peewee Perkins said in the huddle. "Next play . . . twenty-two. How about it, Hal?"

"Just give me the ball," Hal Adams grunted.

Ravenna came out of the huddle with a determined snap that had not been present in past games. They formed the T, with Peewee crouched behind Sweeney. The ball was snapped. Peewee handed it off to Hal Adams. He had nice interference as he started left. Sam took out the Forest end in a perfect block. Turk Bailey boxed the tackle in. Hal cut off tackle, and slanted toward the right. Dennison had taken care of one man in the secondary, and Hal advanced the ball to the Forest 43-yard line before he was nailed.

Hal Adams had made 15 yards on the play, and the Ravenna rooters were so surprised by this sudden display that another play was in motion before they could organize a yell.

Turk Bailey took it on a delayed split, and hit the line for six. Buzz Wilson and Crowell had opened a hole for him.

"Now we're loggin'," Peewee said in the huddle. "Sam, it's your turn. Number thirty-two."

Sam Chambers took the hand-off, and he was gone like a frightened kangaroo. When a Forest tackler got his hands on Sam, the ball was on the Forest 20-yard line, and first down was coming up. Forest called for time out.

"I wouldn't believe it, folks," the radio announcer babbled into the mike, "I wouldn't believe it, but I saw it with my own eyes. Something new has been added to this Ravenna team. I've watched them play all season, but they've never had this drive, this interference, this teamwork. I don't know what Coach Murdock has done to his boys, but whatever it is, it's powerful medicine."

After the time-out, Peewee took the ball on a quarterback sneak for six. Then Hal bulldozed his way through the Forest right guard for five

more. It was goal to go, and Ravenna had the ball on the 9-yard line.

"Let me have it," Sam Chambers said as they formed the huddle, but Peewee shook his head. He called Turk Bailey's number, and the big fullback smashed through the center of the line and bowled the secondary down at the goal. He was over for a touchdown.

The Forest student body, stunned by this unexpected power, sat in shocked silence. Across the field the Ravenna students were screaming in wild hysteria. This was the first time they had seen their team score in such decisive fashion, and their enthusiasm exploded.

Turk Bailey failed to make the try-for-point, and the Ravenna players trotted back to their positions for the kick-off as if making a touchdown was a commonplace event. There was no show of emotion on the part of the Bulldog players. This was a workmanlike thing they were doing, and the job was not over.

Ravenna kicked-off to Forest, and Tod Bayles and Dennison were down with the kick. They swarmed over the Forest receiver, and he was smothered on the fifteen.

Forest tried two running plays that only netted five yards. Their third play was a pass that fell incomplete. They kicked on the fourth down, and Hal Adams caught it on the fifty.

It looked as if the Forest end would cool him off, but Rutledge scampered out of nowhere, and blocked the end out of the play. Adams went for eleven yards.

On the bench Coach Murdock sat weak and bewildered. Usually he paced the sideline, but today he hardly felt equal to it. Of one thing he was certain—whatever was happening on the field was not of his planning. True, he had taught them the plays. He had nursed this team along through failure and defeat, and lurking in the back of his mind was knowledge that it could be a great team if it caught the spark. He had been unable to touch off that spark through seven games—but now the Ravenna Bulldogs were hotter than an A-bomb, and almost as explosive.

Ten yards, six yards, fifteen yards . . . then Peewee on a run-or-pass play heaved one to Sam Chambers who took it over his shoulder in the end zone.

Ravenna scored again in the second quarter and kicked the goal. When they went to the locker room for the half there were 20 points on the board for Ravenna High.

Coach Murdock started to follow his players into the dressing quarters, but when he had covered half the distance he thought better of it. He returned to the bench, and sat alone during the intermission. He refused to talk to reporters.

This team was an inspired team, and Murdock had no desire to break the spell.

The second half was almost a repetition of the first. Forest stiffened in the third quarter, and held Ravenna scoreless, but the Bulldogs broke the Tiger's back in the fourth period, and punched over two more touchdowns.

The last score came on another run-or-pass play, with Peewee taking the ball. This time he decided to run. And what a run! Forty-eight yards through the entire Forest High team. Only one man laid a hand on Peewee, but he was too late. Runner and tackler rolled over the goal line in a tangle of arms and legs, but Peewee hugged the ball tight to his blue jersey.

The final score was 34 to 0 in favor of Ravenna High.

The Ravenna locker room was a bedlam of noise and hilarious congratulations when Coach Murdock walked in after the game. The team gave a spontaneous cheer for the coach, and Murdock just stood there, a big grin on his face, not knowing what to say.

It was not until the excitement had died, and most of the players had left, that Murdock got an explanation of what had taken place.

Peewee Perkins found the coach alone in his office, and he walked in uncertainly.

"I have a confession to make, Coach," Peewee said.

"It's about time," Murdock said, still bewildered. "Out with it, Peewee. What happened?"

"Turk and Sweeney and I figured it out," Peewee said. "I heard the assistant coach from State was going to scout the game. We three were the only ones in non-competitive positions. You know, there are two ends, two tackles, two guards, and two halfbacks. We wrote notes to the men in these competitive positions telling them of the coach's visit, and mentioning the fact he would be watching to see which one played his position better. We figured they would play over their heads. It kind of worked."

"An understatement, if I ever heard one," Coach Murdock grinned. "It was a nice experiment in applied psychology. Thanks, Peewee."

"Aw, it was nothing," Peewee said. He backed toward the door, embarrassed, and collided with a visitor.

"Pardon me," Peewee said.

"That's all right," the stranger returned. "Aren't you Perkins?"

Peewee nodded.

"I'm Townsend," the State coach said, extending his hand. "Nice game, Perkins. When you start planning for college I want a talk with you. We're looking for a smart quarterback."

Colin Lochlons

Scared
Scatback

He looked wistfully at the candidates for the Riverville High football team working out on the practice field. Del Smith wanted to be with them, running and passing and kicking footballs. But Del was sure that he would not go out for the squad.

No use in a fellow like me going out for football, he thought morosely. Remembering the season he had tried to make the team at Central City High, he shriveled up inside. You can't play football when you feel like you're—

"Okay, Buff, let's see you cover this one."

The shout from a husky boy cut through Del's thoughts. The shouter swung his foot mightily against a football. A tall, lithe boy with a shock of buff-colored hair shot erect from a linesman's crouch and raced downfield under the kick.

The husky kicker reminded Del of his cousin, Hal Smith. Del's fingers trailed across the front of the pullover sweater he wore. The sweater showed the outline where a letter C had been removed. Hal had given Del the sweater a month before when he left for the State U. football camp. It had been Hal who earned the letter-sweater, starring at halfback for Central City High.

Blame it, Del thought, why couldn't I have been husky and tough like Hal? Why couldn't I have been built more like . . . ?

"Hey, watch it! Heads up!"

Del jerked a startled gaze toward the shouter. The husky boy gestured at the football he had just kicked. The ball had sliced from his foot. The punt was spiraling toward Del on the sideline. Del made a deft catch of the twisting ball.

In the same instant, he was aware of the tall boy bearing down on him. Del feinted one direction, swerved sharply to the opposite. He tucked the ball beneath the arm away from the charging boy. Del jabbed out his free hand and used the stiff-arm to pivot neatly away, then abruptly he realized that he was interfering with practice. He stopped, tossed the ball to the other boy.

"Didn't mean to butt in," Del said. "Sorry."

"You're sorry!" The taller boy snorted. "A

guy makes me look like a clumsy monkey who never heard of a ballcarrier feinting—and he's sorry!"

He eyed Del. His gaze flicked across the brighter outline on Del's sweater where the C had been.

"I'm Buff Emery," he said. "Haven't I seen you around in the halls?"

Del nodded. "Del Smith," he said. "My folks just moved to Riverville. I enrolled just the day before yesterday."

"Smith, huh?" Buff Emery eyed the C-mark on the sweater again. "Just moved to Riverville, huh? From Central City?"

Again Del nodded. He was a little surprised. The look he gave Del held something close to respectful awe.

"And can we ever use Smith from Central City!" Buff cried. "Jeeps, why haven't you reported out for the team?"

He did not wait for Del to answer. Buff yelled at the boy who had made the punt.

"Hey, Fred, c'm'ere!" Buff went on talking to Del as though he had not interrupted himself. "Happens the guys elected me captain for this year and two things have been worrying me. One is that I wasn't so hot at covering punts last year—

looks from the way you foxed me a minute ago as though I still need plenty of work on it. But I guess being slickered by you shouldn't make a fellow feel too bad. The other thing that made it look as though we might have a rough season was because our star ballcarrier graduated. But with Smith of Central City playing halfback for us, we'll—"

The football captain broke off. He turned toward the husky boy who had come up.

"Meet Del Smith," Buff said. "Fred Lenter, Del. Jeeps, Fred, this is *the Central City High Smith!* And he enrolled at Riverville a couple of days ago!"

The thing hit Del with full force. Suddenly he felt limp and empty inside. This was just dandy. Buff Emery was taking him to be Hal. It was understandable that Buff would have read in sports sheets about Hal's gridiron feats for Central City High. That blamed letter-sweater he had slipped on after school!

"Jeeps!" Buff chortled. "Will we ever go to town with Smith in the tailback spot! Wouldn't surprise me if we kept that old county championship and—"

"Hold up a sec." Del cut in. "You're going too fast. Maybe you'd better slow down."

"Listen to the guy!" Buff slapped Del on the

shoulder. "It's okay to be modest. But after all!"

"Well, look. I'm not even out for the team. I don't intend to come out for the—"

"But you've got to! Jeeps, let's get this thing on the beam. You're Del Smith. Right?"

"Sure. But I—"

"And you're from Central City. Right? It's swell with us that you didn't swagger out here with a Central City letter blazing, but a guy can see where it was before you ripped it off. Okay. Smith, plus moved here from Central City, plus— well, it adds up to a swell break for Riverville High.

"You've *got* to play football for us! We won't take any answer but yes. How about it? We look for you out here in practice gear tomorrow?"

Del hesitated. An aching longing for a place of his own in the football sun struggled with the knowledge that he would be riding on a ticket that Riverville thought was being handed to Hal Smith. Blame it, he hadn't *said* he was the Smith who had been a Central City star. He stifled the shriveled feeling inside. He shrugged, nodded.

"You're in for a big letdown. *I* wasn't the big shot at Central City," he said. "But if that's the way you want it, I'll report for practice to-morrow."

"That's sure the way we want it!"

Buff Emery ran off across the field, bent on

telling the other boys. Fred Lenter stood regarding Del.

"Smith, of Central City fame," Fred said. His tone was flat. He eyed Del. There seemed to Del to be a doubt in Fred's expression.

"Let's have it straight, Smith," Fred said. "I'm trying for the left halfback spot. Whether you're a big-city-high hotshot or not, I'm still trying for the left halfback spot!"

He trotted off across the field.

Del stood in his position awaiting the opening kick-off for Riverville's first game. It was still hard to believe. Less than two weeks before, he had been just a new student at Riverville High. Now he was Riverville's regular left halfback. Little things that had happened flashed through his mind.

"Jeeps, Del, you fake a tackler out of his shoes! Where the heck did you learn to dodge like that?"

Del had pondered Buff Emery's question. Where *had* he learned to squirm and fake and swivel his hips? Sure, after watching Hal run away from tacklers in Central City games, Del Smith had pretended he was Hal in fancy maneuvers in his own back yard. He had made many a make-believe touchdown run there. Wriggling and dodging tacklers. But they were only imaginary tacklers.

To his pleased amazement, he had discovered

that he could run away from real tacklers. His confidence increased as practice went on. Boys accepted him. He was no flash in the pan. Fred Lenter had been shifted to blocking back. Del frowned as another scene came to his mind.

It happened one day in the dressing room. Fred Lenter regarded Del thoughtfully. He spoke in a low tone so that only Del heard him.

"You know, Smith," Fred said, "it's a funny thing. I saw a newsreel shot of the game last year when Central City won the state championship. Anybody would think from the movie shots that Central City's Smith was a husky fellow. At least as big as I am. Did Central City provide players with over-stuffed padding? You don't weigh within twenty pounds of me."

Del had not answered Fred directly.

"As a matter of fact," he said, "I really put on weight during the summer. I weigh one-sixty-six."

"And I would have said the fellow I saw in the newsreel weighed better than one-eighty-five," Fred said. "Funny thing—if it was the same fellow!"

That was the first hint that Fred Lenter was suspicious.

There had been another time in practice scrimmage when a second team player intercepted a pass Del aimed at Buff. The second team boy eluded tacklers until only Del was between him and a touchdown. Del shivered now at recollection of the wincing fear that had welled in him. He had remembered vividly the broken collarbone and the searing pain when he had tackled a bigger boy that time he went out for football at Central City High.

He was physically unable to drive himself for an all out tackle. He just crowded the second team boy until he ran out of bounds. As they lined up for the next play, Fred Lenter sidled close beside Del.

"Smith, of Central City," Fred murmured. "Doesn't seem as though the big-city flash would lack the guts to make a tackle!"

Del moved a couple of restless steps now at the memory. Blame it, three or four times he had tried to work the talk around to where he could let it out that he was only plain Del Smith. He would be just as good a player. He had found himself. The fellows would not hold it against him because—

Phre-e-e-e-e-et!

The blast of the referee's whistle cut through Del's thoughts. The other team's kicker booted a high kick-off. The ball arced toward Del. He fielded it in full stride and flashed a quick glance at the pattern of blocking. A clear lane opened down the right sideline.

Del angled across. A tackler partially slipped a block, lunged at him. Del swerved his hips and the tackler's hands slipped from his pants. Del sped past a tackler trying to cut in from the side. It looked as though he was away for a touchdown.

But the safety man of the other team raced over. He gave ground to lessen the angle. Del saw that he was not going to be able to beat the tackler. Del feinted left, cut back quickly. The tackler was not fooled by the fake. He drove at Del. Just before he would have been hit, Del angled sharply out of bounds.

He railed at himself inwardly. He knew that he might have broken the tackler's effort, surely would have made a few more yards by driving straight.

"The way to go!" Buff Emery slapped Del on the back. The captain clapped his hands, yelled pepper talk. "Del's given us the start, gang. Let's show these guys who's boss right now!"

Going into the huddle, Del knew that Fred Lenter was eying him. A kind of disdain was in Fred's eyes.

"Should have had five or six more yards," Fred said flatly. Definite challenge was in his tone as he added, "Gutless fellows have no business playing football!"

On the second play from scrimmage, Del took the ball in the tailback position. He faked beautifully as though he was swinging wide on an end run and drew the defense over. Then he shot a hard pass diagonally across to the opposite side. Buff Emery grabbed the ball. The captain sped down the sideline into the end zone without a tackler getting closer than five yards. Fred Lenter kicked the point and it was 7-0.

Just before the end of the half, the rival team scored. They missed the conversion try, but Del was not happy. That touchdown was largely his fault. He had missed a tackle and a ballcarrier ran forty yards to the Riverville two-yard line before Lenter spilled him from behind.

So I missed a tackle, Del told himself fiercely. So what? Anybody can miss a tackle. But he knew that he had hesitated a second's fraction before he threw himself at the man. He just could not make himself go all out. Everytime there was that shriveling fear inside.

Between halves Fred Lenter jabbed with the needle again. "It's too bad they stopped the two platoon system," Fred said. "Maybe we could have a *defensive* half in the game as well as a flashy ballcarrier!"

Del flushed. Grimly he vowed that he would make Fred eat his words.

Fred Lenter did double duty all right. In the middle of the third quarter Fred demonstrated that he could block as well as tackle.

Del carried the ball on an off-tackle slant. It was Fred who threw the key block on a line backer to shake Del into the clear. Then, unbelievably, it was Fred who cut in front of Del and threw a crisp block that washed the safety man out of any chance for a tackle. Del carried the ball across the goal line. But he knew it was Fred's touchdown. He trotted near Fred as they went upfield after Fred kicked the conversion try to make the score 14-6 for Riverville.

"Eight of those points are yours, really," Del said. "Two points after and the TD they gave me credit for."

Fred glanced at Del. It was the closest thing to a friendly look Del had ever had from him. But then he merely grunted, giving no reply.

The rival team did not fold up. They received the kick-off and ground away with a line attack. Most of the plays were aimed at the side of the line backed up by Del. They scored a touchdown with two minutes of the fourth quarter gone. They kicked the point to make it 14-13 on the scoreboard.

Darn it, Del thought. They've spotted that I'm a rotten tackler. I've got to slam into them.

He just could not do it. Every time there was an opportunity to smash into a ballcarrier, he funked it.

In the last minute of play Fred saved the game

after Del shirked a tackle. Buff was slickered on covering a punt. The ballcarrier roared down-field. He squeezed past as Del tried to crowd him out of bounds. Fred's desperation tackle from be-hind knocked him off his feet on the six-yard line. In the dressing room, Buff slapped Del on the back.

"Jeeps, am I glad we had you in there!" Buff cried. "That long run put the old game on ice!"

"Yea, man! . . . You left 'em like they stood still! . . . Sure did carry the mail! . . . Two TD's and both of them engineered by Smith!"

Other boys joined Buff in praising Del. Not Fred Lenter. He stood silently, scowling. When the room quieted a little, Fred faced Del.

"We were lucky to hold them to two touch-downs," Fred said clearly. "There *should* be *four* fellows in the secondary defense!"

Buff Emery broke the silence which followed. He glared at Fred.

"Never figured you for a sorehead," Buff said. "Jealous of Del because he beat you out for the tailback job! What are you talking about, any-how?"

"I'm talking about the way Smith chickens out every time there's a tough tackle." Fred eyed Del steadily. "Smith won't deny it—he knows it's true!"

Other boys looked at Del. An air of expectancy

held the dressing room. Del flicked a glance at Fred Lenter, dropped his gaze to the floor.

"It's a free country," Del muttered. "Everybody is entitled to his own opinion."

That dressing room scene was the beginning of friction that threatened to ruin Riverville High's football season. If there had been a coach, he might have worked things out. But Riverville was too small to afford a regular coach. The faculty member who handled the team knew little football. Buff Emery was the real coach. Buff was no fool. What he saw after the first game—and Fred Lenter—lifted the scales of adulation from his eyes. But he did not see them the way Fred did.

"Look, Del," the captain said after the second game. "You scored the winning touchdown this afternoon and we squeaked through. I'm grateful. But—well, the thing is, you aren't so hot on defense. Fred and Blacky have to make tackles on your side of the line. Didn't the coaches at Central City High teach you guys tackling?"

Dell shuddered inwardly. He was remembering an assistant coach at the big high school yelling caustic criticism in tackling drill. He remembered hurling himself at a much heavier first team ball-carrier and the collision against hard-driving knees. Oh yes, Central City taught tackling! But there was nothing he could say.

"Guys are beginning to gripe about it," Buff went on. "Ever since Fred shot off his bazoo. It's no help that you take his needling without handing it back, either."

Del knew deep in his heart that there had to come a clash with Fred. He dreaded it. He tried to rationalize, tell himself that Fred was a bully, a sorehead because he had been beaten out of the tailback job. But it was no go. It bothered Del to realize that he was getting by under a false reputation. And he was more and more sure that Fred knew he was not the Smith who had starred at Central City. Things were bound to come to a head—but the old shriveling fear ate inside him. He cringed at the thought of physical combat.

The fight came in the dressing room following the third game of the season.

The game had ended in a 7-7 tie. Del scored the Riverville touchdown—but he funked the tackle that would have kept the other team from making the tying touchdown late in the game. Fred Lenter called a spade a spade in the dressing room after the boys had dressed.

"I'm fed up," the husky blocking back said. "A fellow knocks himself out blocking for a mug who can run with the ball and that's all. He makes tackles that the mug ought to make. Comes one that the mug misses and nobody can make and—aw! Why don't you give the fellows the real story and stop masquerading as a hero, Smith!"

The room quieted. Del stood up slowly. He said, "What do you mean?"

"You never played football at Central City! You've been riding high down here, playing us for a bunch of backwoods hicks! You're a four-flusher, Smith—and I can prove it!"

Fred reached in his locker. He pulled out a folded paper. There was a picture of a ballcarrier side-stepping a tackler in the paper.

"This is a copy of the *State University News*," Fred said. "I wrote and asked a few questions. This picture in the *News*—and the story with it— answers all of them. Listen."

He read from the paper.

"Hal Smith, freshman sensation who ran wild in his first varsity game, carries on the type of play that made him an All State selection as a senior last year at Central City High. State is fortunate that relaxed eligibility rules make it possible for Smith to play varsity ball as a fresh-man . . ."

Fred's lips curled.

"Masquerading as a hot shot," he bit out. "A gutless four-flusher! Probably your cousin is the same breed and it will come out when the big boys begin really banging him!"

Del clenched his fist. That was hitting below the belt.

"Hal's more football player than a dozen like you," Del said.

He faced the other boys.

"Okay," he said. "I went to Central City High. I went out for the team in my sophomore year and—well, never mind. I never claimed to be Hal. I'm the same guy I was the day Buff talked me into coming out for the team. 'Course I know I should have knocked that idea out of your heads and I apologize for that, but—" He turned back to Fred Lenter. He said, "I think you'd better take back that crack about Hal."

Fred scowled. Something flickered across the back of his eyes. He said gruffly, "Nuts! I don't take back anything I said!"

Afterwards, Del was appalled at what he did then. He leaped at Fred. He swung a round-house right and his fist crashed full against Fred's mouth. The blow staggered the bigger boy. He looked incredulous, as though he could not believe what he saw. Then he said, "You asked for it, Gutless!"

It really was no fight. Fred Lenter outweighed Del twenty pounds. He knew something of boxing and Del knew nothing. Fred's first blow connected with Del's jaw and sent him sprawling. He crashed into a row of lockers. But he was up instantly. He rushed at Fred, thrashing both fists wildly. Fred shook off the blows. He knocked Del down again.

Del got up. He rushed at the bigger boy. Fred Lenter scowled. "Get some sense, fellow," Fred panted. "You couldn't punch your way out of a paper bag!"

Del landed two ineffective blows to Fred's head. Fred crashed a solid fist to Del's jaw. Again Del slammed into the lockers. He was groggy, practically out on his feet. But he struggled up. He stumbled forward toward Fred. Buff Emery caught him, held him with both arms.

" 'S enough," the captain said. He eyed Fred Lenter. "And you called the guy gutless!"

Fred Lenter wore a peculiar expression. He ran his tongue across his lips.

"Smith," he said, "I apologize for the crack I made about your cousin. Maybe I owe you an apology for other things I've thought but—oh, nuts!"

Fred turned and left the dressing room.

Del was thinking about the fight as he waited for the start of the Rock City game. Today he was going to lick the shriveling fear. He was going to show Fred Lenter that he wouldn't chicken out anymore!

But it was not so easy.

A Rock City halfback broke through the line and barreled downfield on Del's side. Del had every intention of meeting him head on—but he funked it. At the last second instead of hurling himself at the ballcarrier, he tried to edge the rival man out of bounds. He failed. The play went for a touchdown and although the try-for-point was missed, Riverville was behind.

Tears of frustration stung Del's eyes. He gritted his teeth. What was the matter with him?

You've got to lick this thing, he told himself furiously. You didn't dodge contact when Fred Lenter knocked you sprawling. You got up from the floor and came back for more. Forget that tackle you tried when you were only a skinny sophomore!

The game went on. The first half was almost at an end when the same rival ballcarrier broke through tackle and roared down at Del. A blocker was in front. It was impossible to edge the ballcarrier out of bounds.

Del gritted his teeth. He found himself giving ground, desperately hoping a teammate would come up to help. But there were no teammates near enough. It was up to Del Smith to stop the play or give the opponents another touchdown.

He did not know that he made a decision. He only knew that abruptly he hurled his body desperately into the air as the blocker threw his block.

Del sailed over the block. It was not really a tackle. He simply collided with the ballcarrier. But they both sprawled to the ground.

Del lay there half unbelieving that he had done it. Buff ran up, pulled him to his feet.

"The way to go!" the captain shouted. "You slickered that blocker like you slicker tacklers. I knew you could do it!"

Del grinned. He felt wonderful. So he hadn't made a clean tackle, he had stopped the guy, hadn't he? Why, there was no more to it than getting up after Fred Lenter had battered him to the floor! He looked around for Fred. The husky blocking back was staring at him. Fred wore an odd look.

It was still 6-0 when the half ended. Scoreboard figures had not changed at the end of the third quarter. Del grew more and more grim. That one miserable missed tackle just couldn't cost his team the game!

"Let's go," he cried suddenly. "We've got to score!"

Fred Lenter eyed him. The husky boy said, "Lead the way, we'll follow—Smith!"

He had never called Del anything but the cold, formal Smith. The biting mockery in Fred's tone made Del more determined.

The signal for Del to carry on the off tackle slant was given in the huddle. He eyed Fred challengingly. "Give me a block," he said. "And I'll lead the way!"

Fred gave him the block. He cut down the Rock City line backer. Del raced downfield. But three men were cutting across to pin him against the sideline.

He had to score the touchdown. He had to wipe out the touchdown he had given Rock City. If only there was a blocker to take one of the tacklers.

"Cut over!" A panting voice gasped behind Del. "Give me a chance to block those fellows!"

Del knew it was Fred. But he also knew if he slowed or cut, one of the Rock City men would smear him. Suddenly he knew what he could do. The old, crawling shrivel curled inside him at the thought. It would be murder to throw himself at those big guys! He drove harder. He wasn't going to make it. He half-turned, yelled, "Take it! I'll give you a block!" He tossed the ball toward Fred.

He threw his body blindly at the two front tacklers. He felt the shock and jar of the collision and then he was tangled with arms and legs and bodies. The jam pile forced the third potential tackler to swerve. The instant he lost gave Fred his vital chance. He cut inside and the grasping fingers of the tackler were brushed aside by Fred's stiff arm. Fred raced on into the end zone.

Fred kicked the point after touchdown. Score-

board figures changed to Riverville 7; Rock City 6. Buff and other teammates pounded Del's shoulders as they trotted upfield for the kick-off.

"You don't need to put out rave notices for me," Del said. "As a matter of fact, flipping that lateral was a reflex action. I had a closeup of those three Rock City bruisers and I didn't want any part of being tackled by them! So I threw the ball any old where. I was scared!"

"Yeah," Fred said. He was looking at Del. There was something about Fred's expression that told Del things were different.

"Yeah," Fred repeated. "You were scared. Scared scatback is what you are—Del!"

Del grinned. He had a comfortable feeling that Fred and other teammates fully accepted Del Smith—as Del Smith.

William Heuman

Bench
Captain

Ben Carver sucked on half an orange. The juice was supposed to give him extra energy for the second half of the game and to replace energy used up in the first half. The only trouble was that with the score tied after a bruising first half, Ben's uniform was unspotted. He was remembering how different it had been last season in this big game when he'd scored three touchdowns, leading the Madison Tigers to a stunning 33 to 0 victory.

Joe Bronson, Madison fullback, tossed his sucked-out orange peel into a nearby carton and said, "You see that right end charging in on that reverse off left tackle, Ben?"

"He's coming in very fast," Ben nodded. "Can't you cross-block him?"

"He's slippery as a chunk of mercury." Joe scowled.

"I noticed you've been going at him too fast," Ben told the fullback. "You've committed yourself too quickly, Joe. You give yourself away, then he knows how to handle you."

Joe thought about that as he scratched the black stubble on his neck. "That could be it, Ben," he nodded. "I've been too anxious to put him out of the plays and as a result he's getting around me."

"You'll get him next half," Ben said confidently, and he noticed how dirty and grass-stained Joe's nylon pants were in comparison with his own. Joe's face and hands were dirty, too, and he had a small cut on his chin, the badge of honor.

His blond hair neatly combed in place, Ben sucked on his orange peel as Joe went off to have a word with Coach Howie Sanders.

Last game of the year, he was thinking. *Last game for Captain Ben Carver of Madison, and he's going out in neon lights, his uniform unspotted!*

Tommy Harrigan, Madison quarterback, slid onto the bench next to Ben. Tommy was a sophomore, moved up earlier in the season from the jayvee team to help spell Ben Carver at the quarterback slot. He'd spelled Ben right out of his position because he was truly a splendid young football player, doing all things well, doing them magnificently. Once Coach Sanders had tried him at the quarterback position, every man on the squad realized that that was where he belonged. They knew, too, that Ben Carver, who had been elected captain at the end of the previous season, would be going in only to spell *him*.

Tommy said anxiously, "They're killing us on the pass patterns, Ben. What do you think's the matter?"

"It's that big No. 8," Ben told him. "He covers a lot of ground behind the line. I'd pass farther out toward the sidelines, Tommy. Tell your receivers that, and then give them a little more time to get out and away from that No. 8 man."

Tommy nodded. "He's tough. I can't seem to keep my passes away from him. Maybe you should be in there, Ben."

"I can't hold a candle to you when it comes to passing," Ben smiled. "Don't be crazy."

He couldn't match Tommy's running, kicking and ball-handling, either, because young Harrigan was a natural, and Ben Carver wondered how they got that way. He'd had to come up the hard way, sweating through the jayvee team, battling for a first string position with the varsity, and then this, his last year, losing out to a sophomore who still had two more years to go.

He wanted to be envious of Tommy, but Tommy Harrigan was as decent a kid as you'd find anywhere, and his great success on the grid-iron, being selected All-State quarterback, hadn't gone to his head.

"If I were you," Ben was saying, "I'd watch those hand-offs, especially to Jackie Brand. He's fumbled once, and he nearly lost the ball in two other very tight spots."

"What am I doing wrong?" Tommy wanted to know.

Ben grinned. "Maybe you're trying so hard to deceive Montrose from that T-slot that you're deceiving Jackie, too. You conceal the ball too long and then you ram it at the carriers, which makes it difficult to handle. A fumble can lose a game like this, Tommy, just one. They won't fumble if you give them nice, soft hand-offs."

Tommy Harrigan rubbed his hands. "Right, Captain," he nodded and slapped Ben's back as he moved away.

They went out on the field for the second half, and Ben Carver sat down on the bench after the kick-off. He watched Tommy handling his team, his powerhouse fullback, Joe Bronson, the two speedy halfbacks, Brand and O'Conner. It was a great backfield, probably the greatest in Madison history, and Ben Carver, captain of the squad, had been unable to break into it.

Madison did better in the second half. Tommy started throwing his passes out closer to the sidelines out of reach of the ubiquitous defensive center. Joe Bronson had learned how to handle the slashing Montrose right end who'd been smearing a lot of their plays. There were no fumbles, and Madison rolled to two touchdowns, but the scores did not clinch the game because Montrose roared back in the fourth quarter for two touchdowns of their own, and they converted both times when one of Tommy Harrigan's extra-point kicks struck the upright and bounced back on the field. It was 27 to 26 for Montrose with six minutes to go, and then Coach Sanders called Ben Carver from the bench.

Ben had anticipated that he would be going in because Madison had the ball on their own thirty-one, first and ten, and Tommy Harrigan looked a little winded.

"Take it, Ben," Coach Sanders said. "Keep rolling that ball for us. No passing. Let Bronson and Brand run."

"Right," Ben nodded and he sprinted out.

There was no great cheer for him because they were all too busy cheering Tommy Harrigan who had played his usual tremendous game, scoring twice, once on a sixty-eight yard run, and had passed for another touchdown.

Joe Bronson said when Ben came into the huddle, "Our Ben. Get us over there, Cap. We've only got six minutes."

"Plenty of time," Ben told them confidently.

"No fumbles. Everything nice and easy. We want short gains through the line, and we aim to hold the ball until we're in pay dirt."

He wanted to run this afternoon because he had great reserves of energy, having sat on the bench most of the season; he wanted to pass, but he wasn't that good a passer, and he wasn't a runner in the class of Bronson or Brand.

He handed off and he called his plays, and he gave them confidence. In the huddles he was cool and poised. He'd studied this game carefully and he'd seen the little weaknesses in the Montrose line, and these he probed, Bronson and Brand making the small gains, but always moving the ball.

They went across midfield, and then down to the forty and the thirty. Then Brand broke loose over left tackle, Joe Bronson slamming the slippery end out of the play on a delayed block, and Brand rolled to the seven.

Ben immediately sent big Joe driving down the middle, and Joe hit to the three. Brand tried the off-tackle spot again, but slipped on the churned grass as he was coming up to the line. Lunging forward, though, he made it to the one and a half.

Time was running out now. Montrose was looking for that big slam through the middle with Joe Bronson carrying because Joe was the powerhouse. The thing to do now was to cross them up on this third down. The natural here was the quarterback sneak.

Ben Carver had visions of himself sailing up into the air, vaulting the Montrose line, landing on his stomach over the goal line for the big score which would win the game. Then the cheers and the back-pounding which would follow.

He wasn't going to do it, though. The quarterback sneak was the play, but it was the play for a tricky, tremendously fast and hard-running quarterback like Tommy Harrigan. Ben Carver started too slowly. He might not find that hole the way Harrigan would, and this play had to go all the way because Montrose would throw eleven men at the runner, and they'd stop him.

Ben knew what the play should be, and he knew that Howie Sanders knew it, also, and Sanders didn't have the heart to take him out. Sanders knew what the second string captain had gone through this season sitting on the bench. Sanders wanted him to have just a little glory these final seconds of the big one, but it was wrong. What was right was to win, and it didn't really matter which man scored.

Unhesitatingly, Ben stepped out of the huddle, looked toward the sidelines and then punched at his right knee with his fist, indicating to Sanders that he wanted to be taken out.

Howie Sanders frowned, watching with his hands on his hips, and then he signaled for

Tommy Harrigan. Ben trotted from the field and he stood beside Coach Sanders, his helmet under his arm, as Harrigan called the play Sanders had given him, and then instead of handing off, vaulted the line and fell into the end zone for the score.

"You didn't have to do it," Sanders said quietly. "You earned that score, Ben."

"I might have missed it," Ben told him. "I knew Tommy wouldn't."

The gun had sounded ending the game, and the eleven Madison men out on the field had turned and were running toward the bench. Tommy Harrigan was leading them, and yelling, "Where's the phony with the bad leg!"

Ben Carver grinned. Howie Sanders said softly, "Don't miss this, Ben. You deserve it."

Captain Ben Carver didn't miss it. They swarmed around him, yelling, hoisting him up on their shoulders, and then they headed toward the locker room with him.

"I played six minutes of this game," Ben protested. "Cut it out."

"You played every minute of every game," Joe Bronson assured him, "and you played it better than any of us. Now shut up. You're rocking the boat."

Ben shut up, but he was happy, supremely happy.

William Hallstead

The Boy Who Threw the Game Away

With four critical minutes left in the season's final football game, Springdale High's captain, Jack Major, called time out.

"We've got to do something sensational," he told his team, "or we'll never win the county championship."

"Harmon Phipps is just too good for us," halfback Glenn Wheeler said. "We hold them for fifty minutes, then *wham!* He boots a thirty-yard field goal for the Lions, and we're sunk."

"That's no way for you to talk," Jack said. "You're supposed to be our secret weapon. You're tied with Phipps for the outstanding player award."

"Only because I'm lighter," Glenn said. "I can

run, but Phipps can block, tackle, kick—"

"Now cut it out," Jack said. "The Bears can win this game, and you can win the outstanding player award. It depends on what we do in the next four minutes."

The water boy and student manager ran off the field, and the referee's whistle shrilled. The Springdale Bears snapped into their huddle.

"We've got three yards to go for a first down," Jack said, "and eighteen to a touchdown. We'll give 'em the fake through center and a pass to Glenn."

The Bear linemen trotted into position and faced the crouching Lions. Glenn pulled in close to center, but as the ball was flipped, he side-stepped wide to his left and drove for the Wear-ham goal line. He saw Jack Major fall back from the pile-up on the line of scrimmage. Jack fired the ball hard and flat.

In the end zone, Glenn leaped and reached high. The spinning ball was snatched from his fingertips. Wearham had intercepted. Number 88 flashed away, headed into clear territory. Har-mon Phipps had the ball.

Recovering from momentary shock, a crowd of Springdale jerseys closed in on Phipps as he pounded across his own twenty-yard stripe. He was smothered in the pile-up, but now the Wear-ham Lions were on the march.

"That was my last play for Springdale," Glenn said as he trotted back into defensive position. "Some play." Some way to end his last season for the Bears.

Jack stabbed his cleats into the sod and crouched to meet the Lions' attack. "The game isn't over yet."

Not quite. There were still two minutes to go. Glenn noted that a deadly silence had fallen around the stands. Over there they were hoping for some kind of a miracle, he knew. The Bears dug in, hope fading, but still determined to fight to the last bitter second.

The big Wearham center snapped the ball. Their quarterback faked a line buck and handed off to his fullback. Phipps faded back to find running room. He snaked away from an off-balance tackler and crossed the twenty-yard stripe.

Good blocking took him to the twenty-five; then Jack Major flew out of the confusion and tackled him cleanly at the knees. Phipps went down hard, and the ball got away from him. Glenn threw himself on it, and every player in leaping distance piled on him. But he held tight, and when the official untangled the heap, he lifted one arm and pointed the other straight at the Lions' goal line.

Springdale's ball again, first and ten. But the down wasn't important—the time was. The Bears had just forty-five seconds to score or lose the championship.

"This is the last one," quarterback Major said in the huddle. "We'll use the 'Desperation Play.' It's going to be up to you, Glenn."

Coach Farwell had thought up this one. Basically, it was a run wide around left end. But there were a few preliminaries required before Glenn got under way.

Wearham's brawny linemen dug their toes into the turf like eager bulls. All they had to do was stop this one play, and the county championship was theirs.

The ball was snapped. Glenn faded back, and Jack whirled, faked a pass, and flipped a quick lateral. Glenn took it on the thirty. Wearham's line was caught off-balance, and Glenn passed the line of scrimmage without trouble and picked up speed. He sidestepped Wearham's fast right end, but the backfield closed in on him. He reversed and faked past a halfback, but he saw big Harmon Phipps gallop toward him on a long cross-field slant.

Glenn gave ground toward the left sideline. Though his pounding cleats ate up yardage, Phipps' timing was better than he'd counted on. Between a last-second touchdown and defeat there was only the onrushing Wearham fullback.

The Boy Who Threw the Game Away

He tight-roped down the edge of the field. The goal line flag was just feet away. Phipps lunged, arms grasping for him like steel bars. Glenn leaped over the diving fullback, but Phipps' hand slapped his left heel.

Glenn stumbled, caught himself, and swept across the goal line. A tremendous shout rose from the stands, and Springdale rooters erupted all around the field. The referee dashed into the end zone and lifted his arms in the signal for a touchdown.

Walking from the end zone with the ball, Glenn found his mind spinning. This was unbelievable! Only he alone, of all the people involved in and watching the play, knew that the touchdown was no good. When he'd leaped over Harmon Phipps, the slap on his heel had knocked his foot just an inch or two out of bounds. But apparently no one had noticed—not Phipps, not the referee or the field judge. Only Glenn himself knew that he had stepped over the field boundary on the last and most critical play of the season.

Should he say nothing and take credit for an illegal touchdown that would make a hero of him? Or should he call the violation on himself and lose the game and the championship for the team, plus the outstanding player award for himself? Either way, it was a tough choice.

He handed the ball to the referee and half a dozen hands slapped his back.

"Man, what a run!" Jack Major said. "You've really put the team on top."

He had everything to gain by saying nothing, taking credit for winning the championship—and of course being a phony hero. After all, the referee was the final judge and he'd already called it a legal touchdown. And how would the school react if Glenn reported himself?

A wild roar came from the Springdale stands. "*Yea, Wheeler!*"

Jack looked at him oddly. "What's the matter, Glenn? You ought to be the happiest guy on the field."

Glenn met Jack's surprised look, then found his own glance drifting to the ground. So that was how it was going to be. He wouldn't be able to look a teammate in the eye.

Suddenly Glenn made his decision. Now he was sure he was right. He turned back to the referee.

"That touchdown was no good, sir. I stepped out of bounds."

The referee was uncertain. "What did you say, fella?"

"I stepped out of bounds on the five-yard line."

"*Glenn!*" Jack Major said in an anguished gasp.

The referee called another official. "The boy says he went out of bounds before he scored."

"I got spilled on that play," the other said. "Didn't see it clearly."

The referee tucked the ball under his arm and pondered. A hush fell over the field, and both teams clustered silently around the all-important man in the striped shirt.

Glenn saw Coach Farwell pace along the sideline and crumple his hat in his hands. This game meant a lot to the school—first chance in five years at the county championship.

The head official made up his mind. He walked to the five-yard line and placed the ball. Then he crouched and fanned his arms back and forth in the signal of cancellation. The touchdown was no good.

A great sick groan came from Springdale backers. The Bears converged in a quick huddle. Ten seconds. They ran into position. Four seconds. Three . . . two . . . one . . .

The flat crack of the timekeeper's gun signaled the end of the game, and Springdale had lost the championship. The dejected Springdale team walked off the field and pushed through the stunned crowd.

"I can't believe it yet," tackle Sam Wilson said to Glenn in the locker room. "You threw away your chance for the outstanding player award, too. I just can't believe it."

Jack Major said, "If you say you stepped out

of bounds, I guess you did, Glenn. But that sure was a tough one to lose."

So he knew where Sam and Jack stood—or did he? The rest of the team were silent, and he took his shower, then dressed without saying a word to anyone.

"What's the matter with everybody?" he asked Coach Farwell as they left the gym. "I didn't *throw* away the game on purpose. What does it cost a guy to be honest?"

"They don't know how to take this," the youthful coach said. "I'm not even sure how to handle it myself. It really hurt to lose that game."

Jack caught up to them as they neared the center of town. He walked beside Glenn and the coach for a block of uncomfortable silence.

"Well, I've got a meeting to go to," the coach said finally. "I'll see you fellows at the victory banquet tonight."

"Some 'victory' banquet that'll be," Jack said as Coach Farwell disappeared down Center Street.

"Look, did I commit some kind of a crime?" Glenn said. "The team acts as if I just gave the game to the Lions. As far as I'm concerned, we never had those six points in the first place."

"Guess you're right," Jack said. "Let's have a Coke and forget it."

"How can I forget it? Nobody will let me."

The gang was making plenty of noise, but when Glenn and Jack stepped into the Milk House, a kind of uneasy quiet settled over the place. Glenn waved at red-haired Nancy Harris in a distant booth, but she seemed to look right through him.

"See that?" Glenn said to Jack. "She tracked me down at home last Saturday to get a write-up for the school paper. Now she won't even look at me."

They sat at the counter and ordered Cokes. "And look at Moke Stanley. He and I were going to check on the yearbook ads this afternoon. He's been just staring at that hot chocolate sign. He doesn't want to talk to me either."

"You're being too hard on everybody," Jack said. "We've never come up against anything like this before. We either won or lost, but we never—"

"Never just gave the game to the other team. Isn't that what you mean?" Glenn said.

"No, not exactly."

"Come on, Jack. Either you think I was right or you think I was wrong. Which is it?"

"Don't force me to make up my mind right now."

"You mean you have some doubts? I thought you were the best friend I had, Jack. I thought if anybody would stand behind me, you would."

Glenn set his glass down hard on the marble counter. "I'm sorry, Jack. I can't . . . I can't finish this."

He saw the door through a blurry mist and rushed out to the sidewalk before anyone could sense the trouble he was having to swallow the lump in his throat.

The only person who could talk about the game without acting as if he thought Glenn had sold it to the highest bidder was his own father.

Mr. Wheeler laid his evening paper on the table beside his chair. "If you think you were right, Glenn, then you did the only thing you could have done. That's all there is to it, in my opinion."

"But that isn't all, Dad. How about everybody else? I didn't really think of how they'd feel."

"In this case, I don't think it really matters how they feel, does it? You were sticking to rules set down to keep a sport from becoming a disorganized scramble."

"That's your opinion as a lawyer, Dad—and as my father. But it doesn't make it any easier to face the guys."

Mr. Wheeler tamped the glowing tobacco in his pipe. "It isn't often easy to face people when you've had to make a decision against their wishes."

"They've got a point, though," Glenn said. "I

over-rode the referee, and he's actually got the final say."

"But you pointed out an infraction of the rules. Wouldn't you report a robbery to the police?"

Glenn slumped in the living room chair. "This wasn't a robbery, Dad. It was just a game."

Before Mr. Wheeler could reply, the hall phone rang and Glenn answered.

"Glenn? This is Nancy."

He didn't want to talk to her after being flatly snubbed at the Milk House. He didn't much want to talk to anybody.

"Glenn?"

"Yes, it's Glenn. I didn't think you'd bother to call me after the way you looked right through me this afternoon."

There was a long hurt silence at the other end. "I couldn't face you, Glenn. Not after what the newspaper staff did just after the game. You won't have to bring over your picture next week."

"You're not going to run the story?"

"I tried, Glenn. I really tried. But Mildred and Sam—"

"Well, they're the editors." He'd given up trying to understand people.

"It's not killing the story that makes me so sick," Nancy said. "We've run lots of stories about you. It's the idea that they killed it just because you did something you thought was right."

"Do you think I was right?"

Nancy hesitated, then in a firm voice said, "Yes, I do."

Glenn spoke softly. "I'm sorry I underrated you this afternoon, Nancy. A thing like this shows a guy who's on whose side."

"Don't talk like that, Glenn. Don't put everybody to the test. Give people a chance to think it over."

"Nobody's given me much of a chance except you and Dad."

"You don't really know."

"How about your editors? It didn't take them long to drop the Glenn Wheeler story."

"You know how Mildred and Sam are. They don't know real news when it happens right in front of them. Forget them. I have. Can you use a reporter on the yearbook?"

"You mean you've quit the school paper over this?"

"I have."

"But Nancy—"

"See you at the banquet tonight, Glenn." She hung up before he could tell her he wasn't going. Not to this year's banquet.

He dropped the receiver in its cradle and walked back to the living room.

His father stood up. "Time to dress for the victory dinner, son. How about it?"

"I'm not going."

Mr. Wheeler stopped in the middle of knocking the coals out of his pipe. "You've never missed a victory banquet."

"This one's different, Dad."

"Just because Springdale didn't win? Don't be ridiculous. You know that we have the banquet for both teams no matter who wins the championship."

Glenn stared at the floor. "It isn't that. I just don't want to go."

His father studied him a moment. "The other guys, huh? Okay, son. That's something you're going to have to work out by yourself. But you won't help the situation by ducking it."

Glenn was silent.

"I'm proud of the Bears and the way you played this afternoon," Mr. Wheeler said. "I guess I'll have to go to the banquet by myself."

Jack Major found Glenn still sitting dejectedly in the living room chair at six-thirty. Darkness had come, and little wind gusts swirled the fallen leaves in the yard. Glenn sat up suddenly and noticed for the first time that it was evening.

"Your dad said you were here, Glenn. What's up?"

"Nothing. Go on, you'll be late for the banquet."

"Come on, boy. What gives? The thing has started already. What are you doing here?"

"Sitting."

"I can see that, but you're not being smart."

"You've certainly changed your tune since this afternoon, Jack."

The tall quarterback leaned against the living room doorway. "I shouldn't have said anything right after the game. I should have kept quiet like most of the other guys did. We didn't know exactly what we thought then. I didn't, anyway."

"Do you now?"

"Get your party suit on," Jack said. "We've got a dinner to go to."

The Wearham Lions were filing back to their seats after accepting the county championship trophy when Glenn and Jack slid into their seats beside Mr. Wheeler. The lawyer nodded at them approvingly but said nothing.

Two tables away, Harmon Phipps grinned at Glenn and waved.

"What's that supposed to mean?" Glenn asked Jack. "That he's glad I won the game for him?"

"Will you pull that chip off your shoulder?"

Dr. Shields, chairman of the Spring County Awards Committee, rose to his feet, and the Hotel Spring ballroom quieted.

"Now we come to the outstanding player

award trophy," the graying dentist said, "and I want to tell all of you that this year we had a mighty tough decision to make. Mr. Davies, Mr. Macklin, all the Spring County football coaches, and I met this afternoon and thrashed this thing out. We're inclined to think you'll go along with our decision."

He paused and a stir of excitement swept through the crowd.

"We had to consider two candidates so close in ratings that until this afternoon we were deadlocked. But today's game decided it for us."

Glenn studied his dessert spoon glumly. He'd hoped that Dr. Shields would simply award Phipps the trophy and not make any painful remarks on the game.

He stole a quick sidelong glance at Jack, but the Bears' quarterback had his eyes pinned on the speaker. Across the big room, Nancy smiled at at him.

But he already knew how Nancy felt. What about the other citizens of Springdale? What did they think of their big promising football star tonight? The town would never forget him. Glenn was sure of that. He was the guy who had thrown away their championship.

"Today something happened," Dr. Shields went on, "something that proves our boys are still interested in sportsmanship, no matter how great their will to win. Today a boy chose to lose the championship rather than win it in what he thought to be a questionable manner."

This wasn't what Glenn had expected to hear. This didn't sound at all like a speech for Harmon Phipps. Suddenly he discovered that every face in the room had turned toward him. He felt Jack's elbow against his arm.

"Hang on, Glenn boy. This is beginning to sound good."

Dr. Shields lifted the glittering ebony and gold trophy. "In behalf of the committee, I take special pride in presenting our award to the county's most outstanding football player and a fine sportsman—Glenn Wheeler!"

It wasn't just applause that broke over the ballroom. It was pandemonium. And there were a lot of others besides Glenn who knew that the shout of approval was far louder than any cheer heard at the football field that afternoon.

Jay Worthington

One-Man Team

The big bus hummed and rolled towards Bainton, carrying thirty-one silent, staring football players. Tommy Krull, undersized Carmell High manager, twisted in his front seat, behind the driver, peering with nervous dark eyes at his charges. Coach Drake was driving his own car.

"They're tied up," thought Tommy, "in knots."

The games they had won wouldn't count, today. Bainton was *the* game, like the final exam after a year's work and worry.

Carmell High would have Don Pascoe's right arm, of course—

Tommy Krull's dark eyes narrowed as they focused on the lean, hollow-cheeked youth sitting a few seats rearward, next to a window. Don Pascoe's gray-blue eyes and wavy brown hair gave him the appearance of a 90-plus student (which he was) rather than of a bullet-passing T-quarterback.

But, unlike his wound-up teammates, Don Pascoe seemed to be gazing at the passing fields with a dreamy, almost bored expression. Wasn't the guy worried even a little bit?

Could a one-man team defeat Bainton's powerhouse?

On second thought, reflected Tommy, perhaps Carmell was a two-man team. For at Don Pascoe's side, eyes closed as if in peaceful slumber, slumped "Road-block" Ed Rhode, the other half of Carmell's backfield strength. The wide-shouldered, thick-waisted Rhode was Pascoe's shield on passing plays, and on defense his joyous linebacking had jolted many a rival touchdown drive to a sudden halt, earning him the inevitable nickname of "Road-block" Rhode.

Pascoe and Rhode would be the heroes, win or lose. They had little to worry about, unless it was how many scholarships they might be offered.

Manager Tommy Krull's scowl deepened. The other players had worked just as hard all season and put out just as much, without all the glory whooping that had come to Don Pascoe. They were good, too, or Carmell High wouldn't be bringing an undefeated record to Bainton.

Why, suppose Don Pascoe should be injured on the first play? Maybe—maybe Carmell could win without Pascoe. How did anybody know? For a wicked moment, the little manager considered tripping Pascoe when he stepped down from the bus. But, no. Apart from the ethics of the thing, Tommy decided that he was being fanciful. Coach Drake would scalp him, for one thing. And if Coach couldn't catch him, the worshipful student body would shred him into confetti if he were to disable the idol of Carmell High.

But it wasn't fair. Here were the others, all good guys, ready to knock themselves out for the team. And there was Don Pascoe, looking bored. And Rhode, sleeping!

Manager Tommy Krull slid lower on his spongy seat and glared at the back of the driver's head.

Don Pascoe lifted his bony chin from his hand, at last, and looked down at Ed Rhode's closed eyelids. Don's lips moved, as if he wanted to smile.

"Ssst!" he whispered, very softly.

The lids instantly quivered, and alert blue eyes rolled towards Don. "Mmmh?"

"Knock it off." Don stabbed him with a sharp elbow. "You haven't slept a wink since you went into that act."

Rhode sat up, grumpily rubbing a meaty hand over his cropped, straw-colored hair. "Okay," he growled. "Thought I might help you relax a little if I looked calm and all that."

"I haven't relaxed since we won last week."

"Last week? You haven't relaxed since the first day of calisthenics."

Don Pascoe grinned, then. They understood each other, these two. They were more than a team. They fitted each other like shoe and sock, like bow and arrow, like—well, like a quarterback and his fullback. Don was lithe, fleet, and a thrower. Rhody, his bodyguard, looked almost clumsy on the field. But Rhody was always in the right place, with a key block or tackle. That was Rhody's game, block and tackle. He loved the contact stuff.

They had come a long way together, he and Rhody. As far as Bainton, anyway. He sighed gently and shifted his feet.

"Uh?" grunted Rhode, turning his head.

"I was wondering what will happen if I can't pass today." He felt Rhody stiffen.

"Can't pass?" The loud exhaust and the hum of the tires prevented teammates from overhearing them, but Rhode's voice dropped to a hoarse whisper. "Why? Is there something the matter with your arm?"

"No, no. I mean, we've been completing too many passes. We've been winning most of our games on passing."

"Oh, you mean their line will be rushing you." Rhode's blue eyes became sober. "I'll be there, Don. I'll hold 'em off—"

"Not all of them, Rhody. You'll get the first man. And maybe you'll get two, sometimes. I've seen you do that. You're the best protection a passer ever had. But you can't hold off Bainton's entire line, Rhody. Remember last year's game?"

"Yeah." Rhody was too good a football man to be offended. He rubbed his ribs, as if he could still feel the pounding he had taken a year earlier. "That was the day I learned about football. That Bainton line!"

Don nodded. He was silent as the bus coasted through Altmont. Next stop, Bainton.

Rhody stirred. "Then you think their strategy will be to rush you on passes."

"What else? Our receivers haven't been stopped. And when you can't stop the receivers from catching passes, you go after the passer. Elementary, Rhody."

"But you gotta pass, Don. We can't beat Bainton with our ground game." Rhody scowled. "We don't even have a ground game without your passing to loosen up the defense."

"You don't mean you believe those crazy newspaper stories about Carmell's being a one-man team?"

Rhode's square shoulders twitched in a shrug. "We have one good tackle, Mike Luman. What else?"

"Good ends," said Don, quietly. "Three of them."

"Good at catching passes," agreed Rhode. "But that doesn't give us a ground game. So we have Mike Luman and good receivers. What else?"

"You."

Rhody snorted. "Let's face it, Don. Without you, we'd have a good, average Carmell team. We might win half our games. With you, we're undefeated."

Don ignored the tribute. "I don't like to believe that, Rhody. I don't know if that kind of a team can take Bainton."

"We'll work it out," said Rhody. "I'll block. You'll pass."

"You'll run, too."

"Me?" Rhody looked puzzled. "I'll stagger a few yards through the middle now and then, to keep their defense honest. Is that what you mean?"

"No." Excitement crept into Don Pascoe's voice, for the first time. "Remember that play Coach wouldn't let us use all season? The screen pass? Coach said to unwrap it today."

"Screen pass?" Rhody's blue eyes cleared. "Oh, you mean that mixed-up thing where I pretend to block the end, but I really let him get through, and then I slide out to the right."

"That's it. Our ends go out, and I drop back as if I'm trying to throw a long pass. Our center, right guard, and right tackle count three, and then they all pull out to give you interference. Bainton's line comes pouring in on me, and I just flip the ball over their heads to you—and away you go."

Rhody nodded. "Say, that one ought to fool them!"

"It's a dream play, if Bainton's line is charging in to rush the passer. You could make plenty of yards, Rhody."

"It might set up one touchdown," agreed the fullback. "I wonder how many we'll need today."

"I don't know . . ." Don peered out the window. ". . . but I guess we'll soon find out."

The bus was slowing. Now it lurched into a driveway, crunched over gravel, and eased to a stop behind the gray brick rectangle of Bainton High School.

The field was a picture in the moment before the kick-off, and the over-sized crowd was hushed in thrilled anticipation. The bulky looking Bainton players, kicking off to Carmell, formed an even, precise row. Carmell's eleven waited opposite, in conventional receiving pattern. The freshly marked boundaries and ten-yard intervals formed a clean white geometric pattern on the green sod, and the blue sky overhead was broken only by a few fleecy clouds.

Then the Bainton line moved forward, the bright new ball glittered in the clear November air, and the harmonious scene erupted suddenly into violent action.

Left halfback Mel Pease received the kick, and twisted his way to the twenty-two before he was downed. Don Pascoe called a pass signal on the second play from scrimmage, after a hand-off to Rip Allen had gained two yards. Don saw some startled faces in the Carmell huddle. Carmell High was a passing team, but his teammates hadn't expected their quarterback to start throwing 'way back here, on the first series. The only player who did not look surprised was Rhody.

Don took the ball from center, faked a hand-off, dropped back. He saw his criss-crossing ends as he turned, but only for an instant. Then a screen of figures towered over him, before he could even lift his throwing arm. Ed Rhode knocked out one of the charging Bainton linemen, but the others came on.

Don retreated, dodging and twisting. Off balance, a moment before he was slammed earthward, he heaved the ball in the direction of halfback Rip Allen, near the sideline. The groan from the Carmell seats told him that the pass was not completed, as he rolled clear of his attackers.

Rhody was also pushing himself off the ground, his square chin thrust out in a kind of stunned defiance. Don Pascoe's mouth twisted in an odd grin.

"Now we know," he said.

"Let me hit the middle," growled Rhody. "I'll teach 'em to come busting in like that."

"Not this trip. I'm calling the buttonhook. Let's show them they can't scare us."

The buttonhook pass was good only for short gains, but was comparatively safe and could help to loosen up opposing defenses. The two ends raced straight ahead, then suddenly wheeled back towards the passer.

The big B's charged again. Don darted a few steps to his right, partly because he was right-handed, but also because big Mike Luman at right tackle made the territory on that side a bit safer from which to operate. Don leaped, slammed a spiral at right end Rossoni, as the latter pivoted. Rossoni seemed to catch the ball in his stomach, and had no chance to run as two defenders bracketed him on the spot.

The buttonhook pass had gained nearly eight yards, but failed by inches to give Carmell a first down. Don was forced to kick. He booted a good one, and the rivals took over the ball on their thirty.

The Bainton team was not noted for passing, but had piled up tremendous yardage on ground plays. Coach Drake's defense amounted to an eight-man line to contain Bainton's power. Ed Rhode and the line-backing guard, Moylan, were stationed close behind the line. Halfbacks Rip Allen and Mel Pease also moved up close on the flanks, ready to turn back end sweeps but alert for passes.

This defense was an invitation to pass, but Bainton chose to rely on ground strength during the first half. This strategy threatened to pay off time after time, as the big backs barreled through for first downs. But something always seemed to interrupt their drives. A fumble and a penalty halted the steamroller on two occasions. More often it was a timely tackle by Road-block Rhode or a break-through by Mike Luman on the short side.

But if Bainton's vaunted ground attack seemed to sputter, so did Don Pascoe's famed passing.

And Don Pascoe was taking a beating. He was knocked down on every passing attempt, as the opposing line kept charging, charging, charging. Nothing dirty. The Bainton linemen were just doing a good job of rushing the passer.

Rhody was taking a beating, too, as a secondary

target. Rhody always hurled himself at the first man through, who usually was also the biggest. Don and Rhody found themselves looking for each other after every pass play, to see if the other was still able to stand. They grinned, at first. But their grins had faded long before the first half ended in a surprising stalemate.

The crowd seemed to love it. Some 0-0 games are dull, but others—and this was one—are brimming with suspense, as if a hidden bomb might explode at any moment.

Coach Drake did not criticize his players during the rest period. The wiry gray-haired coach looked proud, excited. He told Rip Allen and Mel Pease to move back a few steps on defense. Bainton might try to loosen up Carmell's defense, he warned, with some passes.

"But don't get panicky if they complete a few short ones. They'll probably score on the ground, if they score." The coach forced a smile. "I thought we'd need at least two touchdowns today, but now I'll settle for one." His voice trailed almost in pessimism. "If nothing happens, I mean."

But something did happen, mid-way in the third period. Mike Luman disappeared under a pile-up, after breaking up a Bainton reverse. The big tackle was holding his right knee as the other players rolled clear.

"That's all for you today, Mike," said Coach

Drake, gently, after examining the knee.

Don and Rhody traded quick glances. Bainton's line had been tough enough with Mike in there. Now the big team began to roll, penetrating Carmell's ten-yard line for the first time.

Carmell stopped the drive at the eight-yard mark, as Road-block Rhode jammed two line thrusts on successive plays.

Don wanted to try Rhody's screen pass, as his team took over the ball. Time was beginning to run out, he knew. And time would favor the heavier Bainton team from here in. Coach Drake had made few substitutions during the long struggle. Don Pascoe and Road-block Rhode had played every minute.

But the eight-yard line was no place for a screen pass, Don knew. He needed breathing space. A slip or a fumble could mean a safety and two points for Bainton. And two points could be the ball game, today.

He handed off to Rip Allen on the first play, but Rip was stopped at the line. Don called on Rhody for a smash. Rhody ran into a solid wall, too, and gained two yards only by stubborn digging.

Don decided to pass. It was a poor risk, but he hoped to take Bainton by surprise. They wouldn't expect him to pass, back here.

He was wrong.

The linemen were crashing through, as Don Pascoe took the ball from center and darted back. They chased him across his own goal line. He never had a chance to look for a receiver. He dodged and side-stepped, frantically trying to escape from the end zone, and was suddenly hit from—of all directions—behind.

The roar from the Bainton crowd told him that he had been tackled in the end zone for a safety. Bainton was now leading, 2-0.

One-man team?

He was a one-man flop.

"It wasn't your fault, Don," panted Rhody, in a choked voice. "Their whole line came through."

"I should have kicked," said Don. "Now they'll sit on those two points through the last quarter."

Bainton did exactly that. The big team was content to control the ball when possible, taking no chances, moving slowly, waiting for the clock to announce their victory.

Don Pascoe did not complete a single pass in the final quarter. Carmell High gained yards, but only on the ground, on Rhody's churning lunges, hand-offs, pitch-outs, and reverses. Bainton's strategy was obvious—to yield short gains while stopping long passes.

The clock ticked. Now the players on both teams were weary, battered. The crowd waited, tense, expectant. Could there be another surprise?

There could be—for Don Pascoe.

Bainton's kicker booted a honey, high, spiraling all the way to Don, back on his ten-yard stripe. Three figures were already downfield, others were coming.

Rhody seemed to hit two of them. Good old Rhody. Don was digging to his right. But there were too many of them. They crowded him to the sideline. He tried to cut back, but they knocked him out of bounds at the twenty-five.

Rhody was slow coming into the huddle. Don stared at him. Rhody's face was frost-white. Now he was leaning on Rip Allen.

Don gasped. "Rhody. You're hurt."

"I'm all right. Kind of jarred."

But now he was swaying. Don stepped back and signaled to the referee. Rhody was still protesting as Coach Drake led him off the field. The lump in Don's stomach made him feel as if he had swallowed an iron ball.

Smoky Staley came in at fullback. Smoky was a good, average back, perhaps a little faster than Ed Rhode. But he was lighter, and he'd never block or tackle like Rhody.

Don glanced at the big field clock. Two minutes. Two minutes to go seventy-five yards, without Mike Luman or Road-block Rhode.

Bainton would be looking for passes, but Don had little choice.

He called the signal for a cross-over pass. He took the ball, back-pedaled. They were charging him. He ignored them, and jumped high in the air. He didn't care what happened to him. He was going to throw this pass. He had a split second's vision of left end Tunnard, and let go. The tormentors hit him in the air.

A rising cheer that died told him that he had almost hit. Almost. Then he felt pain shooting up his right arm, as he pushed himself upright. He gripped his right wrist as he entered the huddle. His lips were tight against his teeth.

Rip Allen noticed. "Now you're hurt, Don!"

He echoed Rhody's words, without thinking. "I'm all right. It's only my wrist."

"Your throwing arm!"

Rip wig-wagged at the Carmell bench, then at the referee. Coach Drake's top-coated figure moved across the field. Now Don's substitute, Ben Hassinger, was coming, too, adjusting his helmet.

Don knew it was all over, for him, but his mind wouldn't stop working. He grabbed Smoky Staley's sleeve, told him the play he had intended to call next. Smoky blinked, and was voiceless. Then Coach Drake was there, patting Don's shoulder, leading him away.

The crowd gave him a mighty cheer, as they

had done for Rhody. Even the Bainton fans applauded loudly. Why not? Their team was winning, 2-0, and he wouldn't be there to throw any more passes.

Rhody's blue eyes were back in focus, as Don squeezed next to him on the bench. He was squirming, muttering.

"We never had a chance to use the screen."

"We might see it, anyway," said Don. "Right now."

Rhody stared at him. "You mean—?"

"I told Smoky to tell Ben Hassinger it was now or maybe never. Smoky is fresh. He could make some yards."

Ben Hassinger had taken the ball from center, and was fading back as if to pass. Smoky Staley seemed to be brushed aside by Bainton's charging end. Now the entire line was pouring through, chasing Ben Hassinger.

Ben turned and, just before he was engulfed, tossed the ball over their heads. Smoky was waiting, all alone. The red line was behind him as he caught the ball. And now Carmell's center, right guard, and right tackle were moving to the right.

Smoky took off for the sideline like a scared rabbit. Bainton's defending backs on that side were in immediate pursuit, but were soon tangled up in the three-man convoy.

Don and Rhody were off the bench, and Rhody

was screaming what Don wanted to yell. "He's going all the way!"

Carmell's ends had gone downfield as decoy receivers, and now were converging on Bainton's safety man, the last obstacle in Smoky Staley's path. Tunnard lunged, missed. But Rossoni had a clearer shot, and the safety man tumbled over him.

And Smoky Staley, fresh and trigger-fast, couldn't be caught as he streaked seventy-five yards along the sideline for the winning touchdown. Bainton High, without a strong passing attack, couldn't reach midfield again before the final gun cracked, and Carmell was the winner, 6-2.

"We did it!" exulted manager Tommy Krull, in the bedlam of the locker room. "Don and Road-block weren't even on the field, and we beat 'em!"

The little manager hastily ran over to Don and Rhody, slapping each on the shoulder. "We couldn't have won without you guys, of course. You were great while you were in there. Terrific!"

Rhody winced.

"Did I hit the wrong shoulder?" asked Tommy, in alarm. "Is it bad, Rhody?"

"Pulled ligament, Coach thinks. The rest was shock."

"How about you, Don?"

"Wrist sprain, and maybe a small bone in my hand," said Don. "We're all right."

Their teammates crowded around them, mumbling sympathy, telling them how terrific they had been. Don had never seen football players so excited.

Riding homeward on the bus, Rhody rested his stubble-cut straw hair against the seat cushion, and murmured, "I still don't know if it's a one-man team, but I guess it doesn't matter."

Don grinned. "I think it's better this way. Everybody is happy, and everybody likes us."

"That's what I mean." Rhody nodded and closed his eyes, and the tires seemed to be purring as the big bus rolled through enveloping darkness. "Now I can catch up on my sleep."

Jackson V. Scholz

Pigskin Prodigy

It looked like curtains for
the Rams. They were backed against the wall,
that last thin barrier—the goal line. The visiting
Wolverines, savage with the scent of victory, came
from their huddle fast. The Rams braced dog-
gedly to meet the blow. Their fans yelled wildly,
"Hold that line!"

Second down, four yards from another touchdown for the Wolverines, with Jake Bodski, the
human juggernaut, bunching his great muscles
for a blast into the line. The ball was snapped.
Jake Bodski made his try—a fake. The Ram line
stopped him cold, but Bodski didn't have the ball.

The left half, Logan, had it for a sweep around
left end. The Rams' right end, Buck Mercer, had

been soundly blocked. He was on the ground but with a lot of fight left in him. He rolled, made several lightning revolutions, reached out an arm and hooked his fingers around Logan's ankle, clinging with a desperate strength.

Logan kicked free, not in time. A Ram linesman smeared him with a wicked tackle. The pigskin squirted out of Logan's arms. A red-jerseyed Ram whipped through the air to snare it. Jim Foster, quarterback, the Rams' big ace, recovered on the twelve-yard line.

The Creighton Tech rooters verged upon hysterics when they saw their Rams come up with a new lease on life, feeble as it was. The Wolverines were leading 13-7 with a scant five minutes left to play. The Wolverine defense was rugged, and the distance to the goal line was discouragingly long. The fans, however, pinned their faith upon Jim Foster.

So did the Rams on the Creighton bench, who were on their feet now, yelling encouragement to their battered teammates on the field. Roy Talbert was yelling too, but no one paid him much attention, which was understandable. Even Roy understood it.

He was tall, with long legs built for speed and a wedge-shaped torso built for punishment. His hair was sandy and unruly, his features firm but not too handsome. Despite his excitement at the

moment his eyes were shadowed with a deep-set worry. To look at Roy Talbert one would never guess he was a genius, a prodigy in mathematics, with a deep, instinctive grip upon the science which astounded his professors, unaccustomed as they were to brilliant students.

But Roy, at the moment, would have traded a large portion of his brains for a chance to face the Wolverines. Next to mathematics he loved football. He knew, of course, Coach Grady wouldn't send him in. He wondered, just as many others wondered, why Coach Grady kept him on the squad. His role, to now, had been merely that of cannon fodder for the Varsity.

Coach Grady chased the Ram subs back upon the bench where they sat in tight-faced anticipation, pinning their hopes, as did the fans, upon Jim Foster's agile feet and nimble brain. The Wolverines called time out. Grady sent in four replacements. Roy Talbert watched them sprint upon the field, stark envy in his eyes.

When the teams once more faced each other on the scrimmage line, the Wolverine backfield was playing loose, expecting a desperation pass. Jim Foster crossed them up by sending Harry King, fullback, on a slant off tackle. The surprise play was good for fifteen yards. A fake pass and another line play netted seven more. A spot pass failed on the second down. On the next play King bulldozed his way through the line for a first down on the forty-yard line.

The Ram fans bellowed their approval, but the yells choked in their throats when Ray Conlin, right half, remained upon the ground, twisting in pain. The wind had been slammed out of him and he could have a broken rib. He was useless for the remainder of the game. They helped him from the field. He was the third backfield man who had been disabled in that game by the rugged Wolverines.

Coach Grady's face was gray with worry as he looked over his replacements. They were few and ineffective. He made his choice with obvious reluctance. With a helpless gesture of his shoulders he snapped, "Get in there, Roy! And for Pete's sake try to look alive—for once."

Roy Talbert exploded from the bench, grabbed his helmet and sprinted on the field. Elation battled with a crawling fear, a terrible uncertainty. Could he follow Grady's orders? Could he look alive—for once?

His begrimed and battered teammates regarded his arrival with misgiving, frank and open. Jim Foster voiced their thoughts.

"Are *you* the best one he could send in at a time like this!"

Roy kept his mouth shut, joined the huddle and heard Jim rasp, "L-42!"

L-42! Roy scrambled frantically through his mind to translate the signal into coming action. It was all a blur—as usual. He'd have to wait until the play got under way, then pick it up as best he could. When the men took their positions he recognized his spot and stepped into it.

It was a pass formation. On the other hand, it was the set-up for a fake pass. Roy swallowed the hard lump in his throat and gambled on the pass. The ball was snapped. Jim Foster faded, holding the ball cocked behind his ear. The Wolverines came storming in. Roy, with sweet timing, threw a savage rolling block, wiping out a pair of Wolverines who were about to dive at Foster. The play clicked. The pass was good for sixteen yards. Roy had guessed right.

Foster told him grudgingly, "Nice work. Let's keep it up."

Roy guessed right on the next three plays, his highest average of the year. The Rams began to look at him as if he might be useful to them. They had clawed their way to the Wolverine sixteen-yard line, third down with seconds left to play. In the huddle Foster gritted. "This is it! R-17! Now make it good!"

The Rams charged from the huddle to the line

of scrimmage. Roy's brain was whirling like a squirrel cage. R-17! R-17! What did the signal mean?

From the tight formation of the forward wall the play would surely go into the line. But what was *he* supposed to do? It was a safe bet Jim Foster wouldn't let him carry the ball. That's all he could be sure of. He'd have to wait and see.

The play broke. The Ram linesmen made their final surging effort. They tore a wide hole in the left side of the opposing line. Harry King, the ball cradled in his arms, was driving at the hole, and the play was finally clarified for Roy. He was supposed to reach the hole ahead of King, zip through and take out the Wolverine left half.

Roy's natural speed was handy, then. He managed to reach the hole ahead of King, but even as he crossed the line he knew he was behind schedule. The play had clicked with the perfection of a blue print. Every man had done his job—every man but Roy. The way was open to the goal line, blocked only by the Wolverine left half, whom Roy should have nailed a half second earlier—but hadn't. The man was in too close. Roy threw a frantic block which the momentum of the Wolverine made futile. The left half sailed across the block to nail King in his tracks. The final gun went off to end the game.

Jim Foster raged at Roy, "You dumb jerk! You stupid bum! You lost that game for us!"

And Roy had to take it. He had no other choice because he knew Jim Foster spoke the truth. And before the hour was out the whole of Creighton Tech would know the truth. The Wolverines would not have won had Roy Talbert done his part. The Rams would be the victors now, if Roy Talbert had been able to remember signals. For that was Roy's secret, to him a shameful secret.

He could remember intricate equations. He could solve involved mathematical problems in his head. Yet football signals stumped him. The instant he heard one a fantastic mental barrier was raised. He could not remember which of the signals applied to the various plays.

He did all right in skull practice. When Coach Grady outlined involved plays upon the blackboard they were understandable to Roy, because a football diagram resembled, in a way, a mathematical equation. It was the signals that confused him. He could not translate them into action.

He had wrestled with the problem until he was half crazy, and had managed to come up with only one solution which he shied away from in quick panic. His common sense told him to make a clean breast of his weakness to Coach Grady, but his resolution always bogged down in the clutch.

Why? He knew the answer. Pride. He was normal enough to take great pleasure from the fact he was a genius. He derived tremendous satisfaction from his position on the campus. He liked the pleasant kidding that went with it: "Hi, Einstein. How's your fourth dimension?"

So it was pride, just pride that held him silent. He did not dare admit that his amazing brain could not contend with football signals. They'd laugh at him, might even think he had a screw loose somewhere. No, he couldn't face it.

He had to face a lot of other things, however. Up to this point the student body had regarded his football with amused tolerance. He was a poor football player. So what?

It was different now that he had lost an important game for Creighton Tech. There was a certain embarrassed formality in their greetings that sent a chill along his spine. He had let them down and they had not forgotten it. Roy Talbert wallowed in a mire of misery.

Some of the pressure was lifted from him by the approach of the final game against the Badgers of State College. Excitement pushed Roy and his blunder against the Wolverines into the background. The game against the Badgers was traditional and always violent. A win against the

Badgers meant the football season was successful. They were tough this year, strong favorites. Excitement boiled and sizzled on the campus. Roy Talbert felt himself excluded.

He was restless and unhappy on the eve of the big game. For lack of something better to do he started for the railroad station to watch the arrival of the Badgers. A large part of the student body and most of the Ram squad would be there for the occasion.

As he passed through the business section of the small town he became aware that Jim Foster with several of his friends was moving along ahead of him. Roy slowed his pace, having no desire to join them. He was in good position to see the thing which happened with unexpected suddenness.

A big man, rounding the corner of a building, bumped solidly into Jim Foster. Roy recognized the big man, Chug Potter, a local rowdy who, together with a sizable group of so-called tough guys, professed a strong dislike for Creighton students. Potter, accompanied by two of his friends, promptly proceeded to make the most of his accidental collision with Jim Foster. Potter snarled, "Watch where you're goin', football hero, or I'll pin your ears back!"

Jim Foster tensed. He was a fighter, smaller

than Potter but more than able to take care of himself.

Potter shot off his mouth again, enjoying the occasion, confident of his size and strength.

"Maybe I'll take you apart anyway. I think you're yellow, Foster."

Roy saw Jim's shoulders quiver, saw the taut angle of his jaw and the look of readiness on Potter's face. And then, to Roy's amazement, saw Jim step back carefully. He heard Jim's taut voice.

"Some other time, Potter. Not tonight."

Jim turned and started away, taking his friends with him. Roy, in a moment of quick shame, heard Potter's nasty laugh of triumph. Roy came within an ace of trying to uphold the honor of the football team by accepting the job Jim had refused, an impulse knocked suddenly aside by an accurate thought that rocked him to his heels, a wave of understanding which left him slightly dizzy.

Jim Foster wasn't scared of Potter, a fact Roy should have known right from the start. Jim's pride was as great as Roy's, but Jim had swallowed his, impelled by a cause which he considered bigger than his pride—the game against the Badgers on the following day. Jim wouldn't let the team down by risking an injured hand against Potter's skull. Jim had guts.

Roy began hurrying after Jim, scarcely knowing what great force was pushing him.

"Jim! Hey, Jim!"

Jim whirled, his eyes still blazing from his anger.

"What do *you* want?" he demanded harshly.

Roy didn't like the greeting, but he held his temper.

"I can't remember football signals," Roy said bluntly.

"You can't *what?* Who asked you—" he checked abruptly. Jim Foster's brain was geared to rapid thinking. "Hey, wait a minute," he said slowly. "Let's play that record back."

"I can't remember signals," Roy repeated carefully. "I'm supposed to be a hot-shot in math. But I'm nothing but a stupid clown when you throw a football signal at me."

Jim Foster scratched his head and said, "Well I'll be hanged. *This* might be important. Come on, Roy, let's talk it over with the coach. He'll be at the station."

They talked it over with Coach Grady. Grady listened incredulously, then said disgustedly, "I should have figured that one out myself. I *knew* you could play football but I couldn't figure what slowed you in the clutch. It never occurred to me that a brain like yours couldn't handle football signals. I suppose," he added shrewdly, "that if

we gave you each play in the form of a compli-
cated equation you could dope it out."

"Yes," admitted Roy, squirming with embar-
rassment, "I guess I could."

"Could you keep things straight if the play were
outlined briefly to you in the huddle?"

"Yes."

"I'll keep it in mind," Coach Grady said,
turning his attention to the arriving train.

There was no indication that the coach had
given the matter further thought when the game
got under way the following afternoon. The stadium was jammed with rabid, noisy fans. Roy
warmed his usual spot upon the bench, ignored
by everyone, as usual.

The Rams collided head-on with the Badgers,
learning early that the Badgers' power lived up
to pre-game notices. They were big and fast and
smart. Furthermore, their reserves were infinitely
stronger than the Rams'.

Knowing this, Coach Grady shot the works
right from the start, hoping for a lead which the
Rams might be able to protect during the later
stages of the game. The strategy was sound. It
even looked as if it might pan out. Jim Foster's
brilliant generalship and accurate passing arm
gave the Rams two touchdowns in the opening

period. The score was 14-0. The Ram rooters worked themselves into a frenzy.

The Badgers, however, did not fold. They settled down and began to roll. Their reserve power paid big dividends as the Rams began to tire. They battered across their second touchdown in the closing seconds of the half. The try for extra point was good. The score was 14-14.

The Rams were bruised, subdued and worried as they tried to pull themselves together between halves. Roy was in the unhappy role of spectator. No one seemed to notice he was there.

The Badgers came out for the third period looking fresh and cocky. They received the kick-off, moved into high gear and uncorked a devastating ground attack which, in a series of six plays, carried them to another touchdown. They converted the extra tally. The score was 21-14. The Rams fans, shocked by the disaster, yelled hoarsely for their team to come to life.

The Rams obliged—up to a certain point, aided by a psychological change which came upon the Badgers. The visitors, certain now that they could win at will, lost a portion of their fighting edge. They began to coast a bit, unaware of course that they were doing so. The Badgers still did most of the attacking, but the Rams held them scoreless for the remainder of the period.

The Rams did their best to stage an offensive of their own. They couldn't get one started. The Badgers, showing the effect of clever pre-game scouting and shrewd leadership, smothered the Ram ground plays and blanketed their air attack.

The final period got under way with things looking darker by the minute for the Rams. The Badgers started another goal line drive which the embattled Rams halted on the eighteen-yard line with a recovered fumble. It was a lucky break.

Roy Talbert, staring bleakly at the game with dimming hopes, jerked suddenly forward on the bench. His heart slammed violently against his ribs, his breath caught in his throat. Coach Grady stood before him, saying quietly: "Okay, Roy, get in there and replace Conlin on the next down. Don't worry about signals. Just do as Jim tells you to."

Roy jumped to his feet, jammed on his helmet, and almost made the blunder of rushing on the field before the ball was dead. Coach Grady checked him. Harry King plowed into the line for a two yard gain. When the ball was down the coach snapped, "Now!" and Roy sprinted on the field. Noting his arrival, Ray Conlin galloped wearily to the side line.

It was not an inspiring entry for Roy Talbert. He heard the involuntary protesting groan of the

Ram fans. He saw the shocked expressions on the faces of the Rams themselves, as if Coach Grady had sent a cripple into the game.

Time was still in, however. There was no chance for protests or second guessing. Roy took his place beside Jim Foster in the huddle. Jim had a reassuring hand on Roy's arm. Jim snapped, "R-18!" Then swiftly he told Roy, "King fakes off-tackle to the left with interference. You take the ball into the right side on a naked run. Got it?"

"Yes."

And Roy had it. He remembered the play clearly. For the first time in his brief football career he knew exactly what he was supposed to do and what was to be expected of the other men. For the first time his muscles were limber and responsive. His mind was alert. A great exultation flooded through him even though he understood the gamble Jim was taking.

Jim crouched beneath the center. The ball slapped against Jim's palms. He pivoted, pretended to slam the ball into King's belly as the big fullback thundered at the line.

Roy's timing was exact, because he knew, this time, what he was doing. He hesitated long enough to let the play register with the Badgers. They fell for it. Roy drove into motion with split-second precision. He heard Jim's grunt of approval as Jim thudded the ball into Roy's midsection.

The Badger left end, racing in, made a frantic dive for Roy, missing by a whisker. The Badger left tackle had been taken from the play by the Ram right tackle and right end. The way across the scrimmage line was clear.

Roy made the most of it, moving at high speed, watching carefully. The Badger backfield, recovering swiftly from its first surprise, was tearing across to intercept him, hoping to pin him against the side line.

Roy permitted himself to be herded as if his only thought was to get as far as possible before they pushed him out of bounds. The strategy paid off. The Badgers, in full cry, were caught flat-footed when Roy changed direction with the twisting motion of a flying bat. The safety man was too far in. He, with the others, plowed to a startled halt and swerved back to protect the center of the field.

Roy crossed them up again with another lightning change. He whirled back toward the side line which was open now. Uncorking everything he had, he sped along the narrow corridor. The safety man got close enough to throw a tackle. His hand slapped heavily against Roy's leg. Roy staggered momentarily, then regained his speed.

He was five yards ahead of his pursuers when he finally crossed over the goal line.

The Creighton fans went wild. The Rams themselves were too amazed to offer any but the most confused congratulations. The try for extra point was blocked. The score was 21-20, a body-blow to the Rams' hopes at this stage of the game. They were still unwilling to accept Roy as a valuable addition to the backfield. So far as anyone could tell, his long run was just a lucky break.

The Rams began to change their minds after they had kicked off to the Badgers. The Badgers started a grim attack, keeping to the ground, unwilling to take the risk of an intercepted pass. They appeared completely confident they could protect their lead.

Their offensive took on power, then ran head-on into a new defensive barrier in the Ram backfield, Roy Talbert. Roy himself could not quite understand it, except that now he was assured of grasping the Rams' attacking strategy, the attacking strategy of the opposing team became clear also. It didn't make much sense, but there it was. His mind, unfettered by the mystery of football signals, was free to grasp the other details of the game.

He seemed to know where the Badger plays

were coming, and he was in there fast to plug the holes with crashing tackles. The effect upon the other Rams was prompt. The tired line stiffened with new hope. The Badgers were forced to kick. The Rams took the offensive.

And Roy Talbert was the powerhouse in the backfield, the new and constant threat. He played with the joyous ferocity of a man who had finally found himself. He was no longer ashamed to have each play explained to him before it started. He was proud to be a member of the Rams.

And they were proud to have him. They proved it with their complete cooperation. Stiffened with new hope, they riddled the Badger line. The Badgers poured in fresh reserves—and held. They played Roy for the dangerous man he was. Time after time they dug in grimly to protect their slender lead. The game was drawing to a close as the shadow of the stadium crept across the gridiron.

With forty seconds left to play the Badgers were in possession of the ball on their own twenty-yard line, third down, six yards to go. The Ram fans tried gamely to be hopeful, but a despairing note had found its way into their yells.

The Badgers stalled too long and drew a five yard penalty. They finally sent the play into the

line. The runner had a hole. It looked for an awful
instant as if he'd go for a first down. He didn't.
Roy hit him, blasted a shoulder to the Badger's
mid-section with a savagery which dislodged the
ball. The pigskin skittered toward the side line on
the ground. A Ram recovered it before it left the
field. It was on the twenty-two yard line. Jim
Foster promptly called time out. There was time
for one play. He glanced toward the bench, but
Coach Grady was not sending the place kicker on
the field. The distance was too great and the angle
was too bad. Grady was leaving the decision for
the final play to Foster's judgment. Jim told the
weary Rams "We'll try L-12." Then to Roy,
"They're expecting a pass. I'll fake it. You cut
across behind me and I'll pretend to sneak the ball
to you for a right end sweep. Then I'll snap the
ball to King who hits off tackle to the left. Got
it?"

"Yes," said Roy surprised that he felt no resent-
ment over not being given the important assign-
ment for the final play. He could see the shrewd-
ness of Jim's move. When the Badgers tumbled to
the fake pass they would undoubtedly accept the
fact that Roy would be carrying the mail in the
Rams' last desperate effort.

The referee called time in. There was dead
silence in the stadium. The teams moved tautly
to the line of scrimmage. The ball was snapped,

and the violent impact of charging men was loud upon the air.

Roy did his part. The timing was exact. He sprinted for the end, pretending to hide the ball against his thigh. The deception worked. The Badger defense closed in to pull him down. Then some Badger yelled a warning, high panic in his voice.

The defense swerved back toward King. Roy flashed in across the line, cutting back toward the zone of action. Harry King was having trouble. His defense had petered out. The Badgers had finally solved the play. It looked as if they had King trapped.

Not quite. A red-jerseyed thunderbolt sliced in. The thunderbolt was Roy Talbert. A pair of Badgers waiting in King's path went down beneath the blasting force of Roy's block. King side-stepped like a cat, avoiding the massed tangle of arms and legs. A long dive carried him across the goal line. The final gun went off before he hit the ground. The Rams missed the try for extra point. Who cared?

Roy Talbert left the field surrounded by his grinning teammates. He had never known this feeling of great happiness and satisfaction. He had made the grade upon the gridiron. More than that, he had solved a problem, and a big one, the problem of false pride. This was proved when Jim

Foster told the Rams, "We've got a half-wit on our team. He can't remember signals. What a dope."

And Roy Talbert took it as a compliment, one of the nicest anyone had ever paid him. He grinned at Jim and said, "Give me the cube root of nine hundred eighty-two."

Jim grinned back and said, "Aw nuts."

Jay Worthington

Hard-Luck Haggerty

Phil Haggerty's grayish eyes rolled nervously, watching his Mapleboro teammates straighten their line for the kick-off. Hurry up, he thought. Blow the whistle, before something happens.

"You finally did it, Hard-Luck!" grinned Spook Tooker, at Haggerty's left. "You're starting against Verdan!"

Haggerty held up crossed fingers. He wasn't superstitious, but—

There. The whistle shrilled across the white-striped field, and the line of Mapleboro jerseys moved forward. Pete "The Barrel" Buna booted the new, yellow football into the clear, frosty November air.

Phil Haggerty sprinted forward. He'd made it, at last. The Verdan game. He hadn't been stricken with appendicitis, at the last minute, or fallen over a bench. Today, perhaps, he could throw off that nickname—Hard-Luck Haggerty. Perhaps his luck was changing.

Or was it?

Pete Buna's kick had hooked toward the sideline, and the ball almost bounced out of bounds at Verdan's thirty-yard stripe. Mapleboro's left end, Faraday, raced straight down the left line, turning back the Verdan flank. The Verdan ball carrier cut toward the middle. He was soon buried, but he was already at the forty-yard mark.

The Rams of Verdan High were almost at midfield, before running a play from scrimmage!

Haggerty's lean face twisted in a scowl. Would his very presence jinx the team?

Local sportswriters had been predicting for three years that Phil Haggerty would be All-County, or leading pass-receiver, or most valuable this-or-that. He had almost believed them, at first.

True, his long arms and fingers, teamed up with his sprinter's speed, made him dangerous on passing plays. There was always that extra threat that, after snatching a pass from the air, he might dash all the way to the goal line. Coach Ambler had patterned much of his split-T offense to exploit the halfback's pass-catching talents.

But Haggerty had cracked his collar-bone in October of his first season. And last year he had broken a bone in his ankle in Mapleboro's opening game. He had yet to complete a season for the Mapleboro Tigers.

So, he had become "Hard-Luck" Haggerty. And as Haggerty went, it seemed, so went the team. Mapleboro High had lost to Verdan those two years, without him.

His teammates didn't blame him for getting hurt, Haggerty had assured himself. But they seemed to think he was brittle-boned. They eyed him nervously, after bruising plays, as if fearing that his luck might again rob them of the championship they could win by downing Verdan.

And now the first break had gone to Verdan, already, on the weak kick-off. The big rival team gained eight yards on two quick dive plays, operating from a balanced "T" formation.

But the second break came Mapleboro's way. A Rams back fumbled behind the line, on the third down. Verdan managed to recover, but decided to kick.

Haggerty was back, waiting to catch the punt. As right halfback he ought to be defending the right wing, he knew. But Coach Ambler had given strict orders for him to play the safety position.

"I want you at safety to capitalize on your

speed," the coach said. "You may be able to run back some kicks."

More likely, Haggerty suspected, Coach Ambler was trying to protect him from contact plays. He was given the softest blocking assignments, and the coach quickly sent in a substitute whenever Mapleboro enjoyed a comfortable lead. Quarterback Spook Tooker seldom called Haggerty's plays, except the passes. The coach, as well as his teammates, seemed convinced that he was fragile, a brittle-bone.

Haggerty hated this pampering, although he was forced to admit that the system had been working pretty well, up to the Verdan game. Mapleboro had been tied once, but they had not been defeated.

And Haggerty had become the celebrated pass-catcher, at last, that the experts had decided he ought to be. He had caught four touchdown passes and snagged many others. Once again the sportswriters were thumping their drums to acclaim Phil Haggerty an All-something-or-other.

Haggerty didn't like such publicity, either. He didn't believe a player ought to be All-anything, if he could do only one job well, such as catching passes. He had seen too much football to be impressed by the All-teams.

"All-baloney teams," he growled to Spook, after seeing one adjective-splattered column about himself. "I wouldn't catch many passes if you weren't hanging the ball up for me."

More important than the personal angle, however—Haggerty was afraid that the headlines, added to the coach's coddling, might put him on the spot. A smart team like Verdan could add one and one together, and decide that Hard-Luck Haggerty was strictly a pass-receiver. Stop Haggerty, stop Mapleboro.

He'd soon know. The other games wouldn't mean a thing, if the team lost to the Rams.

The Verdan kicker had booted a high one. Waiting for it, Haggerty crossed his fingers. He had caught hundreds of punts without a miss, in practice. But he couldn't help wondering if his hard-luck jinx would make him juggle this one.

He glued his eyes on the ball, without looking to see how many opponent figures might be charging at him. He made the catch, but was dumped almost in his tracks, back on the twenty-two.

His fears were being confirmed. These Verdan players were big, fast, and smart. He couldn't believe that a one-man passing attack would beat them.

Spook called for the basic hand-off and dive plays in the first sequence. Mapleboro slowly punched through the grudging Rams line to midfield.

"Now we can open them up!" Spook called one of Haggerty's pass plays. "Get the glue on your fingers, Hag!"

Haggerty broke from his flanker's post, in Mapleboro's split-T. He feinted towards his right, then cut back. Glancing over his left shoulder, he saw the yellow cowhide spiraling towards him. Spook's pass was right on the target.

But Verdan's defense was all ready for him.

Two figures were bracketing him. One of them slapped down the leather, just as Haggerty's itching fingers were closing around the ball.

"Hard luck, Hag!" chirped Spook in the huddle, unwittingly using the nickname.

"It wasn't luck," growled Haggerty. "They're looking for a pass every time I go out. I never do anything else."

"They can't stop you!"

But "they" did stop him, again, when Spook called for another pass on third down. Mapleboro was forced to kick.

Verdan took over. Starting back on the twenty, the big Rams eleven launched a sustained ground march, crunching out one first down after another, until they had crossed the goal line for the first touchdown.

The try for extra point was wide, but the score-

board announced: MAPLEBORO—0. VER-
DAN—6.

Haggerty couldn't catch a pass until nearly the
end of the first half. Spook Tooker used up most
of the second period in probing the alert Verdan
defenses, calling the dives, trap plays, counters,
and a variety of passes.

Then, with about a minute remaining in the
half, Spook found the right one.

It was almost a lateral type of pass. Haggerty
darted straight ahead for a few steps and then
angled sharply to his right. Spook threw the ball
so that Haggerty could make his catch turning to
his right, away from the rival team, reducing the
danger of interception.

The teams happened to be near the right sideline on this occasion. Spook threw his pass higher
than usual, knowing that Haggerty would be almost at the line. He calculated expertly, as usual.

Haggerty was only a step from the sideline
when he went up in the air. Verdan's defensive
back could only wait for him to come down. The
rival defender couldn't get in back of Haggerty
without going out of bounds, and he couldn't risk
bypassing the receiver with a forward leap.

Haggerty saw his opponent's predicament. As
he made his catch and dropped to earth, Haggerty instinctively stepped back towards the cen-

ter of the field. Then, pivoting and straight-arming the stationary Rams figure, he raced straight down the sideline.

In motion, Haggerty could outspeed almost any rival. He was a sprinter on Mapleboro's track team. He was free, already, except for Verdan's safety man, who was desperately legging towards him. Haggerty faked him ten yards away and sped across the goal line without being touched.

The pass had traveled forward only a few yards, but Haggerty had raced forty yards for the touchdown. The Tiger fans shrieked during the run, and again when Barrel Buna place-kicked the extra point.

The first half ended with the Mapleboro Tigers leading by that slim margin: MAPLEBORO—7. VERDAN—6.

"That's the one!" exulted Spook, jogging towards the dressing room at Haggerty's side. "They can't stop that pass at the sideline!"

"Don't count on it!"

Haggerty wasn't thinking about his hard-luck label, right then. He was thinking that Verdan's coach and team could devote the rest period to devising some defense against the play.

"Hurt your ankle, Haggerty?" asked Coach Ambler, anxiously, when he saw his halfback on a bench, rubbing his left foot.

"No, just a cleat scratch."

Haggerty grinned, then sighed. He didn't like to think that the team's fate might be hanging on his pass-catching—or his bones. He'd always be known as Hard-Luck Haggerty, he sensed, if the team should lose this game.

"Try that pass at the sideline again," Coach Ambler was instructing Spook. "That one looks like our best hope."

Spook nodded eagerly.

But Spook didn't get many chances during the third quarter. The second half had begun as a bruising, jolting repetition of the first. Determined to rub out the one-point deficit, the Verdan team controlled the ball with another long, grinding march. The Rams assault was halted once, by another fumble. But then, after a brief exchange, the advance was resumed.

Haggerty was making more tackles now, as the Rams backs crashed into the Tigers' secondary territory. He ignored Spook's anxious eyes, as he hurled himself at the attackers. This was the last half of his last game. Saving his bones wouldn't help now, he reasoned.

Verdan's second touchdown was scored, ironically, on a pass. Barrel Buna had scrambled back into Haggerty's zone, possibly with some notion of protecting his teammate. The Verdan receiver made his catch unmolested, in the opposite corner.

The try for extra point was messed up again,

although now it seemed of little importance. MAPLEBORO—7. VERDAN—12.

The game went into the final quarter before Spook could jockey the team into a spot for the sideline pass. A weak Verdan punt finally gave Mapleboro the ball near midfield.

Spook handed off to Barrel Buna for a dive, and then called for the pass.

"This is the one!" said the quarterback.

Haggerty crossed his fingers, as he crouched in his flanker's post. Verdan's defense would be waiting for the play, he knew. What would they do?

They let him make his catch, without interfering, as Spook tossed another bulls-eye. But two figures were waiting there, when he came down. One was in front of him, at the sideline, and the other was angling towards him. He tried to sidestep, but they boxed him and knocked him out of bounds.

"They're playing it safe," panted Haggerty, in the Mapleboro huddle. "They're giving us a few yards on the play, to stop a long gain."

"I don't blame them!" Spook sighed unhappily. "Now, what do we do?"

Haggerty scowled. "Try throwing it lower. I might be able to fake a cut-back, if I don't have to jump for the ball, and then run the chalk-line."

Spook nodded. "We'll try it. I'll aim at your shoulder."

Spook tried a quarterback sneak on third down. He missed his first down by inches. Now it was last down, with the ball still only a few yards past midfield. Trying for the first down was a risk, but Spook took the chance. His teammates nodded approval. Anything was a risk now, with Verdan winning, and with the clock running out.

The big Verdan line converged to stop Buna's drive, but the sturdy fullback somehow barreled through, and the Mapleboro fans whooped.

"Another six inches and I couldn't have made it," grunted the beefy Buna. "Come on, Hard-Luck. Get us out of here!"

"Yeah," agreed Spook. "Let's end the suspense."

He called for the sideline pass. Haggerty inserted a double faking motion, squeezing all possible percentage from his effort, and then streaked for the sideline. He could see two Rams backs moving parallel with him and the Verdan safety man edging cautiously over.

Spook hit him at the shoulder, as he had promised. Haggerty was able to make his catch on the run. He cross-stepped, faking the cutback. The rival figures scrambled towards him.

He stopped dead, caught them off-balance for a split moment, and then wheeled back to the sideline. One Verdan arm grabbed at him, before Haggerty could gain momentum, but he tore loose.

His legs flashed faster and faster. Only Verdan's safety man, once again, was ahead of him. But this time Haggerty had a helper. His left end, Faraday, was slanting towards the Verdan safety man. Even if he didn't make a clean block, Faraday would delay the rival back long enough.

And then, as the white lines moved under his digging cleats, Haggerty heard a horn. He didn't stop or slow his mad dash. A penalty might favor Mapleboro, he knew, and then the touchdown would count. But something was wrong, back there.

He crossed the last line with the crowd's roaring in his ears and looked back.

The field judge, conspicuous in a striped shirt, was standing on the sideline, pointing at the ground, near the point where Haggerty had begun his run.

Haggerty slowly retraced his route, while Mapleboro's cheering melted into a deep groan. The field judge showed Haggerty cleat marks crossing the sideline. He had stepped out of bounds, declared the official.

Haggerty said nothing. The marks could have been made by the Verdan man who had grabbed at him, but—

He had almost forgotten. The jinx had been slyly waiting for this most crushing moment. He was Hard-Luck Haggerty.

Spook Tooker was yowling at the field judge, red-faced. Haggerty grabbed the quarterback's jersey by the elbow and dragged him towards the huddle.

"Save your breath, Spook. We can't score that way."

"Their halfback was the one who went over the line!" howled Spook. "I saw him!"

"It's only second down," said Haggerty, "and we gained about five yards on the play."

Spook blinked. "You've got a point there . . . . All right, gang—let's dig!"

They did pretty well, squeezing out a first down, and then another. But then the heavy rival line stiffened as the Tigers edged into scoring territory and took over the ball.

The rival team seemed content to protect their lead, with only minutes remaining. They stalled, using conservative plays, and finally kicked.

Haggerty waited for the punt, back of the fifty-yard stripe. It was a high one, and he saw the Verdan ends coming at him. He should have signaled for a fair catch, perhaps, but this didn't seem to be the time to play ostrich. He grabbed the ball, put down his head, and pretended he had Barrel Buna's legs and weight.

He bulled through one of Verdan's ends and ripped away from the other. He staggered, still digging. He sidestepped a third tackler, and was just moving into high gear when two more Rams tacklers hit him simultaneously, one from each side.

He bounced up, ignoring the sudden dizziness, and saw that he had landed the ball on the enemy's forty.

"Hey," croaked Spook, whose face was spotted with welts and grass burns, "I thought you were a brittle-bone!"

"You can call my reverses now," muttered Haggerty, glancing at the field clock. "There's about two minutes left of this season!"

"Okay!"

Spook called on Buna for a dive and then named Haggerty on the reverse. But the play was rusty. Haggerty was juggling the ball as he took it from Spook. He tried to tuck it into his left arm, but his luck was following him. The ball rolled clumsily from his clutching fingers. He dove at it and recovered, but for a loss.

"Sorry," he growled. "Guess I've forgotten how to run with the ball. All I can do is catch passes."

"We'll use the sideline pass, then," panted Spook, "after Buna gives us a first down."

The Barrel's legs churned frantically, but Buna couldn't make the first down.

And now it was last down—and last chance. They wouldn't touch the ball again, Haggerty knew, if they lost it now. Their rivals would stall again, until they ran out the clock.

"Throw it to Haggerty," rumbled Buna, in what might be this Mapleboro team's last huddle.

"Yeah," agreed the quarterback. "The sideline pass."

"We can't work it again," said Haggerty. "That's the one they'll be expecting."

"It's last down," groaned Spook in despair. "What else can we do?"

"Wait!" Haggerty was staring at Faraday, the left end, across the huddle. "That was a nice block you gave me, Faraday, when they called back my run. What were you doing downfield?"

"I'm only a decoy on the play," said Faraday, shrugging. "I didn't have anything else to do."

Haggerty nodded. "Let's do it this way, Spook . . . ."

Haggerty faked as usual, when the ball was snapped, and slanted towards the right sideline. The two Verdan secondaries were coming along with him. The Rams safety man was moving over. The crowd rumbled. Everybody at the game could see the play developing—or thought they could.

Spook was moving behind the line, faking a run and then straightening. He cocked the ball in his right hand, aiming towards the right sideline. Spook's fake was so artistic that, for a frightened moment, Haggerty was afraid he actually was going to get the pass.

Then Spook calmly wheeled and fired a high one towards the left corner. Faraday, who had been drifting right, suddenly reversed his direction. The ball was leading him, and Faraday made his catch without breaking stride. The Verdan safety man had not been caught napping, but he was a step behind all the way. He hit Faraday about two yards out, in a futile dive. Their forward impetus carried both players across the line.

Buna place-kicked the extra point to make the score 14-12. Verdan's team couldn't complete a pass in the few remaining seconds.

"That was a sweet play, Spook," yelled Coach Ambler, above the dressing room uproar, "but I don't remember practicing it. What happened?"

"Haggerty wanted to be the decoy."

The coach turned to the red-faced halfback who had improvised the play and slowly nodded. "It figures. Haggerty was the better decoy, at that moment."

"I thought I ought to stay out of the play, anyway," said Haggerty, grinning, "with my luck."

"Your luck?" The coach shook his head, smiling. "You hang onto your nickname, Haggerty. Anybody who can take bad luck, twist its arm and use it to dope out a new play—well, you'll get along, Haggerty. You'll get along."

Hard-Luck Haggerty's grin widened to his ears.